Justice On The Rocks... Twist

By

Jack Radtke

GRANDPA & GRACE
BEST Wishes
'02

ISBN: 1-4033-2823-4 (Electronic)
ISBN: 1-4033-2824-2 (Softcover)

This book is printed on acid free paper.

1stBooks – rev. 04/29/02

Foreword

Appropriate criminal punishment varies with the mood of society and can be said to be a reflection of society's values. Sometimes, however, these reflections become distorted and more accurately resemble the view found in fun house mirrors.

A rapist is sentenced to twenty years yet serves less than three. A murderer is released after only five years of a life sentence, while in the next state another murderer is executed after an eighteen year delay. An unemployed father, convicted of stealing food for his family does, in fact, serve the entire eight years to which he had been sentenced.

From these inequities change is born. The law, like a bon-sai tree, grows according to the will of its caretaker and reacts to pruning, trimming, adjusting, until, once more, it reflects the values of those it serves.

1.

It surprised him to see his fingers tremble as he traced his name on the envelope. He had waited a very long time for this moment and now that the moment had arrived, he felt intimidated. Instead of opening the envelope, he placed it inside his shirt, next to his skin.

It remained there during his afternoon class, itching, sticking to his skin, begging to be opened.

He found he was unable to concentrate. The professor lectured on but his own thoughts remained with the truant envelope.

At dinner he had fingered the envelope through his shirt, but still refused to brave the contents. Afterward, he studied till past midnight, aware that finals were next week. He unbuttoned half the buttons on his shirt and then pulled the shirt over his head, glancing at his roommate's sleeping form in the next bed. The envelope stuck to his skin.

He sat on the edge of his bed, opened the envelope and pulled the contents out, but sat staring at the folded letter for an inordinate time. Finally, with a deep breath, he unfolded the damp instrument.

"YESSS!!!"

All he had seen was the salutation and the words 'You have been accepted... '.

His room mate sat bolt upright, a pained expression on his face, and obviously confused. Pat nearly shouted. "I've been accepted to Law School!"

When Pat took the time to finally read the entire letter he found there was a string attached. A proviso. The acceptance was contingent upon his ability to present a brief to the university not later than the fifteenth of August. The subject was to be his understanding of the justice system in the United States. Final acceptance would depend, in great part, on his ability to understand that system and to express his thoughts in a manner that would be pleasing to the entrance board. I'm doomed, he thought.

"For somebody that's just been accepted to law school you sure look like you lost your best friend," his room mate said.

Pat explained what would be required to complete the deal.

"What the hell. Your old man's a lawyer. Get him to help you out," his room mate said.

"No way! We haven't agreed on anything since I was sixteen. We barely speak to one another."

While his room mate slept, Pat lay awake staring at the ceiling and wondering how he would complete the tremendous amount of research that stretched before him and write a respectable brief in little more than four months.

That Sunday he called his mother with the news. She was overjoyed, of course. In typical motherly fashion, she could see no problem with getting the brief written and was convinced Pat would set new records with the admissions board and afterward, in all the classes that stretched before him.

Pat implored her to speak on his behalf with his father.

She agreed and that afternoon his father called, but instead of agreeing to provide any help, spent the better part of a half hour trying to talk his son out of law as a career.

Later that evening, Pat explored the campus library and found only one book that seemed helpful but it was nearly a hundred years old. It was a start, though, and he checked out the book and headed back to his room in the dorm. When he arrived, he found a note taped to his pillow. It said his mom had called and he was to return the call as quickly as he could.

"Mom? You called?" Pat said.

"Yes. Was Dad able to help you out?"

They spent nearly an hour on the phone, and in the end, Pat was astounded to discover he had a great grandfather. Of course, he knew he had a great grandfather. He was just surprised to find his great grandfather would still be alive. And better yet, he was not only an attorney, but something of a legend in law circles. The only drawback was that the old man was a bit of a recluse. No one in the family had seen or heard from him in years. Prior to that, with his reputation for being a crotchety old man, the family preferred not to talk to him anyhow. Pat's hopes had risen and been dashed in less time than it took for the auto-dialer to dial his home number.

His mother was quick to assure him that all was not lost. She would do everything she could to locate the old man and make arrangements for Pat to call him.

It was two days before she called with some news.

"Well, he's every bit as cantankerous as your father had always said, but he's willing to take your call. Providing you've got the guts to call and don't waste his time. Those are his words, not mine." She gave Pat the number and wished him luck.

3

The next morning at nine sharp, Pat made the call.

Damned unusual to need an appointment to call your own great grandfather, he thought as the connections were being made.

When he heard the deep gravelly voice for the first time he was unable to speak immediately.

"So. You must be Pat. I can spare you just six minutes. No more. What is it you think I can do for you?"

His voice was clear for his age, but was made rumbling with the years that had passed and, no doubt, from thousands of courtroom confrontations. Pat used a little more than two of his minutes explaining his dilemma but was cut off abruptly by the old man's piercing interruption.

"In my day, we researched our own briefs, young man. I'll not be a party to this."

Pat, unable to contain his surprise at this lack of civility, was struck speechless for a moment.

"If you're to be a man of the law, you should be able to respond and respond quickly," the old man said. "You've less than two minutes left and you're wasting them. See if you can answer this: Why do you want to study law and why should I help you?"

"Because I love the law and I'd even be willing to put up with a miserable old bastard like you to do it."

Pat had originally intended to stroke the old man's ego to convince him to help, but in a fit of anger abandoned that plan.

A deep, rumbling laugh started down at the level of the old man's toes and finally sprung from his face, looking as worn and as cracked as old leather when he smiled.

"Boy, you may have possibilities! I'll let you know."

Still laughing, he broke the connection, leaving Pat in his dorm room, dumbfounded.

There was no reason to continue studying. Finals were upon him and if he didn't know the material by now, more studying was unlikely to help. He worked through the night, packing his belongings. In three days, he would have his bachelor's degree and no matter what the future held, he would be out of here forever. First light had not yet broken when the old man called.

"Boy, here's the program. I've cleared my calendar for next week. You be here Sunday evening. I want to know what you're made of. Spend a week. By Saturday, I'll either invite you to spend the summer for an education you're unlikely to get anywhere else, or I'll spend Saturday afternoon giving you enough information to form the basis of your brief. Clear?"

"The whole summer? I can't just... my girlfriend, I have to..."

"Listen boy, if I decide you're worth the effort, it'll mean you won't have time for a girlfriend! Do yourself a favor. Dump her! Be here by seven. I won't hold dinner for you." And just as abruptly, the old man's voice faded leaving Pat wondering what the hell he was getting into.

At his mother's instructions, he packed two weeks worth of clothes, shipped everything else home, and was at the Los Angeles airport for a flight that was scheduled to leave at six Sunday morning. The flight landed in Detroit on time. From there, he took a rented car for the last two hundred plus miles to the old man's cabin.

Pat arrived shortly after six. While waiting for someone to answer the door to the old and rustic cabin, he stood with his back to the door and admired the small lake surrounded by majestic pines. The air seemed cleaner here and everything was so green. So far, he liked what he saw, even if it was substantially cooler here.

"You're early. Long as you're here, might as well come in." It was a grumpy old woman who had opened the door for him.

"Put your bag in the hall. Sit anywhere. Dinner will be ready soon," she said.

She left him in a pine paneled room. Looked like those pictures of studies he had seen. Old rooms with old leather furniture, lined with old books. Cozy, but everything seemed out of place. Like he had stepped back in time.

"Evening, Pat. Dinner's ready. You can wash in there."

"Great grandfather. It's good to meet you."

"Listen, boy. I didn't call you great grandson so don't you call me great grandfather. You're Pat and I'm Al. Just plain Al... or if you prefer, A.J. Now wash up. Dinner's getting cold."

Pat was struck by the old man's bearing. He was shorter than Pat but carried himself as if he were very tall. Even dressed in an old woolen shirt and baggy cords he had presence.

His face seemed weathered and the seams around his eyes and mouth made his face look like soft worn leather. His eyes were dark brown and were covered with shaggy untrimmed brows. He had jowls, which gave his face a squarish look, and his lips were heavy and moist, as if he had just finished drinking something.

He's formidable, now, Pat thought. Imagine what he was like forty years ago.

2.

Pat was in bed. The window was open a few inches and a crisp wisp of air passed his face occasionally. It was only nine o'clock. He thought of his first day with A.J. God, this is weird, he thought. His dad, in the only words of wisdom he had to offer, had told him to take notes and to keep a diary.

He jumped out of bed and started across the room.

He fumbled with the switch on the bedside lamp. A sparse forty watts barely illuminated the room. The ancient pine paneling seemed to eat the light. He found his overnight bag and rummaged through it. The diary. Digging deeper, he came up with a pen.

"Arrived today in time for dinner," Pat wrote. "Met the old man. Wants to be called 'A.J.'. Madge is the housekeeper and cook. She's as nutty as he is. Ate dinner in silence. When we finished, I helped Madge with the dishes and A.J. turned in. Don't know if I'll last the week. Feel the same as I did the first day of college—orientation week. But I was totally disoriented. Maybe if I hang in there, it'll get better."

At 4:30 sharp, Madge was tweaking his nose. "A.J. won't like it if you sleep the day away, young man!"

Before Pat realized what she had said she had disappeared. Fighting to get his bearings, he had two thoughts in rapid succession: It's not even light, yet; and, who the hell was that?

He jumped into his clothes, grabbed his shaving kit and stumbled to the bathroom he had used the previous evening to wash. Splashed some cold water onto his face and ran a comb quickly through his hair. His eyes were bloodshot. He stood leaning against the sink with straightened arms, staring at the running water swirling down the drain. Finally, he slowly straightened, stared at his reflection in the old mirror, and began to shave.

I look like death warmed over, he thought. His sandy hair was in need of a trim, his eyebrows, bushy under the best of circumstances, seemed to grow in all directions. He was good looking—at least his mother told him so. Tall, too. He had to bend over to see his reflection.

His name was shouted so loudly he thought someone must be in the room with him. He quickly recovered and gathered up his gear, ran from the bath and saw A.J., red faced, glaring angrily at him.

"Told you, five!" A.J. said.

A.J. turned abruptly and made for the far end of the hall.

Had A.J. been younger, Pat thought, he would have been storming down the hall, but at his age, it was more like angry teetering. Pat quickly dumped his things on the bed, grabbed a notebook and walked quickly the way his great grandfather had gone.

"Boy, I didn't expect you would be lazy," A.J. said.

"We have an agreement, sir. You prefer A.J. I accept. I prefer Pat, not Boy!"

The old man smiled. "Very well. Pat. This isn't a day for serious talk, anyhow. Thought we would spend it getting used to the place. Show you around.

Jack Radtke

Let you know what the rules are. I think we can stay friendly for an hour or two, don't you? Pat?"

Still smiling, he turned his back on the young man and stretched his arms wide, as if to embrace the room. "This is my study. It's where we'll probably spend some long hours. Although, weather permitting, I sometimes am moved to drift about the lake in my boat."

The room was paneled in knotty pine planks which had turned a burnt orange with age. Along the widest wall, which stretched the width of the building, were six windows, three each flanking a stone fireplace. The fireplace looked well used. On the narrow walls were an assemblage of framed artifacts and many books, most bound in leather. The north wall had two windows, the south wall, three. The entry was wide, perhaps six feet. To the left stood an ancient, but miniature, roll top desk upon which sat the latest in computer hardware and communication devices. There were piles of disks and stacks of paper everywhere.

The rest of the room seemed comfortably furnished with a love seat, two chairs, a couch, an assortment of tables and lamps, and an exercise machine.

"Well, what do you think?" A.J. said.

"I think I expected something different. More books. I don't know. Maybe a stuffier place. It looks comfortable."

"It is. As for books," the old man pointed toward the computer. "That's all the books I need."

He spun about and embraced the room from which they had come. "This used to be a dining room. It's a what-not room now. Just a place connecting the other

10

rooms. That's my bedroom, and yours", he said, pointing first toward a door on the left side of the north wall, and then toward a second door to the right of first one.

A.J. spun quickly around. When Pat turned, he saw the kitchen they had eaten in the night before.

"Madge will be back here about noon. From that time on, the kitchen is off limits. My bedroom", A.J. gestured over his shoulder, "is always off limits."

"C'mon." A.J. left the "what-not" area and headed into a short hall opposite the study. He gestured to his left, "Bathroom," and to his right, "Laundry."

Directly ahead was a door leading outside, but not the same door through which Pat had entered last night.

A short walk led them to a small log building. A.J. pulled open the door. It creaked, but left the impression that it might have been the old man's bones creaking.

"Wood storage." A.J. said. "Used to be the main cabin before the house was built."

Pat leaned into the building. Dirt floor, a two hole crapper to the right, the remnants of a sink with exposed, rusted plumbing at the back wall. One small window over the sink, a bare bulb hanging from the open rafters, and a hole in the roof with a rubber bathmat covering two thirds of the hole.

A.J. shook his head. "Been meaning to tear this down for the last thirty years. Oh well, makes a good storage shed."

They walked around to the south side of the main house and looked at a single car garage. A.J. didn't offer to show Pat the inside, and Pat didn't ask to see it. From where they stood, the lake was visible to the south and to the west, in the pre-dawn gloom.

The water was cool and clear. A small dock jutted out into the water and tied to the dock was a small rowboat. Pat stood on the dock with his back to the lake looking up at the house. Sure seemed larger and more forbidding last night.

Just like the first days at college, he was beginning to feel at ease. When he turned back to his great grandfather, the old man was sitting in the boat, at the stern.

"You row", he said.

3.

A.J. handed Pat an old fishing pole which had been rigged for crappie. "Catch us some lunch."

Pat had never fished before and was surprised to feel a vibrant tug in his hands.

"Pull him in, boy! Oops, sorry. Bring him right in here, Pat."

The fish was small, about the size of Pat's hand. A.J. put the fish into a screened contraption that hung by a cord over the side of the boat.

"We'll need about a dozen of these, so keep on bringing them in." A.J. said.

After the third fish, A.J. started a conversation. "So what is it about the law that seems so fascinating? Are you going into it for the money? Are you an idealist? Want to lock up criminals? What?"

Pat was hard pressed for an honest answer. He just didn't know. In fact, the decision to pursue law sneaked up and surprised him. When he entered college, he had in mind being a teacher. Then, while signing up for courses in the beginning of his third year, he suddenly just knew he would someday be an attorney. He didn't know how to explain that, but the look in A.J.'s eyes demanded an answer.

"None of the reasons you suggest," he finally said.

"But I don't know myself how to explain it. I think I might be intrigued by the process more than the result. And when I think about it, I guess criminal law seems more interesting than other options, but I don't know if I'd prefer to be on the defense side or the prosecution side. Every case I've read about... well, I can visualize myself giving either argument."

During the silence that followed, Pat could hear distant birds chirping.

"There's one more thing," Pat said. "When I helped my dad - you know, in divorce cases - I always hated to have him ask me to look up old cases to support his position. But then I'd get into it, and I'd be so fascinated by what I would find that dad would have to come looking for me and tell me to stop. I've worried some about the confrontation, too. I don't know if I can stand up to another attorney in front of a judge, a jury, and, worse, the client! What if I turn into a mumbling idiot? What if the other attorney found laws that support him perfectly and I walk in thinking I'm going to do a great job and my premises turn out to be worthless?"

"If you become a lawyer, at least a good one, those doubts will pursue you forever," A.J. said. "Time enough to worry about that. In the meantime, I'm interested in what motivates you to even try."

Pat thought for some time before answering. "I guess I like the system. It's logical. And I want to use that system to be a winner. I guess I don't think much about the people involved. I mean, who of them will win or lose. They seem like bystanders in a great game and I want to play the game... to win the game!"

He thought for another minute or two. "Sounds pretty shallow, doesn't it?"

"Yes. Yes, it does," A.J. said. "I'll venture that you wouldn't find many practicing lawyers that would admit such a thing but, Pat, that is exactly what drives most of us to enter the field and in fact, to keep playing the game. They prefer to say 'I love the law' or some such thing, but what they're really saying is the same thing you've said."

A.J. held up the basket. "Looks like lunch to me."

While Pat rowed in, A.J. filled him in on something he had never heard before. "Your dad doesn't love the law! That's why he's a miserable bastard. He never has and likely, never will. He went into it because his father was a lawyer and it was expected of him.

"Then he began to think about the money. There's several ways for a lawyer to get rich, and most of them require the lawyer to be good at what he does. No, better than good.

"Most trial lawyers—criminal lawyers—make peanuts.

The ones that are good get their names in the paper and leave the impression that all lawyers get rich. Not true. Your father knew that. He also suspected he wouldn't be good enough.

"Next best would be corporate law. Also a dog eat dog world. He didn't think he would be good enough there, either.

"Then there's divorce law. Any schmuck can make out in divorce law—words of wisdom from your father. Amounts to taking the client for everything he's got. If you have rich clients, you make out pretty well.

"Your dad picked that career simply because he didn't think he would be good enough for anything else. And the saddest thing is that he would have been good enough. What he lacked wasn't brains. He lacked passion!"

The boat bumped the dock.

Pat couldn't help thinking, you think my dad is a miserable bastard? What about you?

It was true. But what right did this old man have to say it?

As if A.J. had read his thoughts he said, "I suppose you're thinking I'm a crotchety old bastard, too?" But he smiled as he said it.

Pat didn't answer, but the look on his face was all the answer A.J. needed. "You may be right, Pat. Part of it is my age. When you get to be this old, it's part of your God given rights to be as crotchety as you've a mind to be." He chuckled for a minute or two then continued. "I've practiced a special brand of law. There's only a few of us who do. As a result, my work has alienated both friend and family. As a result I've many times have had to ask myself if I still loved what I did. I did and I do. Enough to give up the pleasures of family and of friends. Oh, I have friends. But only a few. And they're not the kind to spend idle hours socializing, but they're there for me when I'm in need, as I am for them. Special relationships. Then there's a few others, like Madge. I wouldn't classify them as friends, exactly. Just friendly acquaintances. But, I don't need to defend myself. It was they that banished me."

He stood silent for a moment, looking out over the lake. "Let's get these fish cleaned."

The old man cleaned the first two, then turned the knife over to Pat. Not having ever tried this before, Pat struggled with the job but ended with some respectable pieces of meat. A.J. took the knife and demonstrated how to strip the filet of its skin and Pat finished the job.

A.J. rinsed the meat under running tap water and Pat objected to the blatant waste of running water, to which A.J. said, "It's my water."

A.J. placed the filets over a screen rack and fitted the rack over a pan of boiling water. While the fish were steaming, Pat set the table and A.J. made a sauce of catsup and horse radish. When served, the meat had broken into small pieces. A.J. dolloped some of the sauce over the fish and served them with warm rolls and white wine. Pat preferred the fish without the sauce but tried it both ways. As simple as it looked, this had to be the best meal Pat had ever tasted.

"You clean up. Time for my nap. Make sure you're out of there before Madge shows up." As A.J. crossed the what-not room, he slowed to a stop and cocked his head as if considering something. He turned back. "Let's just hold up on the clean-up for a moment or two. How do you feel about an impromptu aptitude test?"

"OK. I guess."

"Good!" The old man re-joined Pat at the table.

"Here's the situation. A small group of youngsters are milling about in front of a theater. A popular children's movie is playing and they're trying to talk the clerk into letting them sneak in to see it. 'Shoo,' says the agent. 'Get out of here!' The children step away and are talking among themselves. Meanwhile, an elderly couple, standing not far away, watches the development with some interest. They approach the agent. The gentlemen reaches into his pocket and pulls out a money clip and counts his cash. Still holding the money clip he says to the agent, 'I'll tell you what. Why don't you count the kids as they enter?' The agent waves the children forward and counts them as they pass the turnstile. As the last one enters, the gentleman says, 'How many was that?' The agent replies, 'I counted twelve.' The gentlemen fingers the money in his clip, pulls out one dollar and hands it to his wife, saying, 'Well dear, you were right and I was wrong.' With that the elderly couple turn and walk away."

Pat was smiling broadly.

"Amusing story," A.J. said, "but here's the test part.

The theater owner is upset. He goes to the police. The police are unsure what to do. They take it to the prosecutor — that's you.

"Take the next couple hours to think things over. When we get together this afternoon, be prepared to tell me if you would prosecute; why; based on what law; how you would make the basic argument; and whether you would win. And of course, you don't have to cite case law. Just use your common sense."

Pat was still smiling as his great grandfather left the room but now his smile was twisted, as if to remark on the old man's humor.

He thought about the test case, almost in spite of himself, and after vacillating for some time, decided to take it seriously and respond accordingly. The elements seemed to be there for a crime, but who would be charged? A.J. hadn't specified that. The guy with the money? The kids? The agent? This was a little more difficult than it had first appeared. Pat eliminated the agent. He had been duped, pure and simple. The kids could be charged with something, but there was no way to win a case against a bunch of kids, so it would have to be the old couple with the money.

Now, what's the charge? It was clearly a scam and maybe thievery. After all, the theater owner rightfully expected to make a legitimate profit by charging to see a movie and due to the actions of the man with the money clip, he had lost some of his earnings. Nope. Didn't feel right.

How about… the guy with the money is a con artist?

Feels right, but what about motive. He doesn't gain anything. But maybe A.J. hadn't spilled everything he knows. Maybe it's all about a grudge. That's it. I'll have the guy getting even with the theater owner for some past grievance by cheating him out of the price of a dozen tickets.

With that, A.J. came out into the yard where Pat had been pacing with his test problem.

"A real poser, isn't it?" A.J. was clearly amused.

"Well, let's hear it. Will you accept the case?"

"Yep!"

"What's the charge?"

"It was a con game. A scam. I don't know what the legalese is for that, but that's the charge."

"Okay." A.J. drawled the two syllables out slowly. "So you're charging the man and his wife. What's your argument?"

Pat went on for some time, creating 'facts' to back up his theory that the couple had been faulted by some previous action of the theater owner, and in a premeditated manner screwed him out of his money.

"Hmmm. Did you win?"

"Yep," Pat said.

A.J. was silent for some time. He rubbed his chin and stared off toward the lake. Pat tired of waiting and finally blurted out, "How'd I do? Did I pass?"

"Not a pass or fail situation. Unless of course, you really were in a courtroom for this exercise. Anyhow, this is only half the test."

"Oh, man." Pat was disappointed in the old man's games.

"The other half is this. I lied before. You're not the prosecutor. You're a defense attorney. The real prosecutor accepted the case and has charged... well, use the same scenario that you used when you were prosecuting. Will you accept the case? If so, what is your defense? And, most importantly, will you win?"

"I don't see how the..."

"Ach, ach, ach! Not now. Think about it. I have some work to do and don't wish to be disturbed. I'll see you at dinner. While you're thinking, feel free to fish or just wander around. It's beautiful country, and don't worry, you can't get into much trouble around here. Just don't get lost."

Pat stood immobile in the yard for some time, wondering where his great grandfather got this crap! His mood was interrupted by a noise on the far side of the house. Walking over to investigate, he discovered a rental car agent coming to retrieve his car. He spoke with him for a few minutes and got the number of the local agency so he could call at the end of the week for a pick up. He was that sure that this whole project wasn't going to work out.

At dinner, Pat didn't bring up the test and neither did A.J. In fact, Pat thought that maybe he had forgotten. Most of the conversation was about life in the north country with A.J. doing all the talking. If Madge heard anything that was being said, she didn't show it. When the meal was complete, A.J. took Pat out through the front of the house for an hour or so of enjoying the evening.

"Bound to be a fine sunset," A.J. said.

They sat on wicker furniture on the front porch. From here they couldn't see the lake, but they could hear loons screaming their crazy calls.

"So. Pat. Did you accept the case?"

"I don't want to, but in the interest of finishing this test I'll say yes."

"Sounds like your enthusiasm has waned."

"I just don't see the point, that's all."

"May not be one," A.J. said. "But we won't know that till we've finished. What will your defense be?"

"That the entire episode occurred in innocence. The couple made no offer to pay for the kids, only asked the agent to count them. They settled an innocent betting debt and left. The agent and the owner read more into the situation than was there by any stretch of the imagination. The kids couldn't be faulted, since they were waved forward by the agent. If there was a fault anywhere, it was with the agent who presumed that an offer to pay was being made, which of course, was not the case. Move for a dismissal."

Pat felt a little smug.

"What about the plot to get even?"

"Probably the facts would not hold up under cross, since the prosecutor made up the scenario to provide motive for his case. Since this is my test, I'm claiming

I'm good enough at cross examinations to make the prosecution's witnesses, if any, fold. And, if there are no witnesses, I'm also pretty good at summation. I'd get him there, so I win!"

A.J. didn't respond. In fact, it was unclear if he had even heard the answers.

"So what does this prove," Pat said. "Do you think a made-up case will make or break me? Is there any 'right' answer?"

"Well Pat, I don't know if there is a right answer or not. It was a real case, though. I was the prosecutor. Almost thirty years old and I had a righteous attitude. By God, that charlatan would pay his dues! I took the same approach that you did when you were playing prosecutor."

All of a sudden Pat was intensely interested. "Did you win?"

"Don't know. All I can tell you is what happened." A.J. seemed to be reliving the case. "I stood before the judge, spoke my piece, much the same as you outlined it, except I was a little more animated. I had justice on my side, you know."

A.J. sat silent for a few moments, remembering the events of over a half century ago. "Anyhow, the judge was red-faced and I took that to mean that he was as outraged as I.

A glance at the defense table worried me a bit. My worthy opponent was placidly sitting there, smiling. Finally, the judge gathered himself up till he looked seven feet tall, then he came down on me. And I mean hard! Told me about wasting his time, the court's time, my own time... I was so embarrassed. The counsel for the defense continued to smile, but now he was busying himself with some papers. I think he was embarrassed for me. The case was dismissed. All the way down the hall, the theater owner was shouting at me, everyone in the hall was watching. I couldn't get away fast enough."

"Wow! How could you keep practicing?"

"Oh, it took a little while for my pride to heal. But I muddled through with some help from a friend. One of my law professors was in the courtroom that day with several students. He used that case in his classes for years afterwards, damn him.

"But the important thing is that he also called me, took me to dinner and explained how a more seasoned professional might have handled it. It wasn't too late. I took his advice and things worked out well."

"Well?" You can't just leave me hanging here. What advice? What did you do?"

"I went to see the old couple," A.J. said. "Asked them why they did what they had done. There was no malicious intent. They just wanted to help out some kids and they thought the few dollars involved wouldn't stack up to a hill of beans with the owner. They promised to avoid such Robin Hood activities in the future. Then I went to see the agent. Told him that if he followed some simple rules, like sell the ticket before admitting anyone, the whole situation could have been avoided. He agreed and apologized. Mostly for getting me chewed out in open court, I suspect.

"But the best part was when I talked to the owner. He was pretty grumpy in the beginning but I convinced him to use this experience to his advantage. The following week he ran an ad that said every Saturday, at the matinee, he would select, at random, ten children to see the movie free. From then on, till he died, the line on Saturdays was nearly double the length it used to be. As for me... I learned you could love the law and still be human about it."

The sun was nearly completely down now. They watched the afterglow in silence. Finally Pat asked, "How did I do?"

"That's up to you to determine. I just wanted you to see what you're getting into. If the gentle stuff doesn't scare you off, maybe we'll talk about my later career some day. By the way, if you can generate the same enthusiasm for the defense that you had for the prosecution, you might just be a fine lawyer. Think about it." The old man rose and entered the house. "See you at five."

4.

Leroy called his shot and made it, but he scratched.

His opponent laughed, swaggered around the table and said, "Rack 'em. You're buying again."

They were talking about getting laid. They were both liars. Leroy, barely twenty one, claimed enough conquests to enable him to qualify as a moderately successful gigolo. His pool partner was able to keep up. Since quantity made no impression, Leroy was providing intimate details, most of which he had read in the magazines — the kind kept behind the counter at the pharmacy. The fact that his opponent seemed to believe him was probable proof that he had little or no experience himself.

In truth, Leroy's total experience had been limited to three times, but in his own mind, coming close counted. The first occurred when he was eighteen. His date was grossly over-weight. They were in his pickup at the river, he with his zipper down, she with her tights and panties around her knees. Penetration never occurred, but neither of them were aware of it. They panted and heaved, grappled and moaned. But the closest he came was stroking against folds of fat. As a result, he celebrated by drawing squiggly little sperm on his fogged windshield while the girl quietly cried and worried about being pregnant. They never saw each other again.

The second girl was a hooker. She knew penetration when it occurred. He ended up taking penicillin but thought it was worth it.

The third instance was rape. Not the kind that would be reported, but it was clearly not by mutual agreement. The girl had thought she might have led him on. In her desperation to get away from him afterward, she remembers telling him how good he was and that he should call her. When he did, she wouldn't talk to him. When he arrived at her home, her mother said she wasn't home but he could see her watching from an upstairs window when he drove away. He didn't know what the problem was, but he was sure that she wanted him again.

After weeks of unsuccessful attempts at seeing her again, he began cruising her neighborhood in the evenings. On a Saturday night, he happened to drive by just as her parents were getting into their car... and all dressed up.

He circled the block and parked three houses down from hers. Sneaked up to the window and peeked in. Through the sheer drapery liners he could see her on the couch. She was polishing her toenails and occasionally looked up at the TV. She wants me, he thought, and there's no interfering parents around.

He knocked on the door and stepped back to the window to watch her approach. The robe she was wearing was loose and he could see most of one breast. Then she wrapped the robe more tightly about herself and reached for the door. He stepped over and when the door opened, he said, "Hi, baby. What's happening?"

She started to close the door but he already had his foot inside. She started to yell but it never occurred to him that she wasn't happy to see him. He reached for her and snatched the robe from her shoulder. She was back-pedaling fast. He managed to pull her toward him and tried to kiss her, all the while thinking how excited she was to see him.

She brought her knee up hard into his groin. He was half doubled over and his eyes were as big as saucers. She drove a bony fist into his solar plexus, knocking the wind from his lungs. He nearly collapsed. She was still charging and screaming. He stumbled backwards out the door across the porch and fell into shrubs which had short but very sharp thorns.

When he began to recover, still in pain but able to walk if he stayed bent over, he looked through the large window again and saw her loading a gun.

His memory of that encounter varied greatly from the facts and he counted that among his many conquests.

It wasn't that he wasn't a good looking guy. He was just short of six feet but thin. He wore his hair a little longer than the other guys, his jeans were always dirty and he wore them low on his hips. None of the girls had ever seen him without his engineer boots which looked too heavy for those thin legs. No, he was by no means physically unattractive. It was more in his presentation. He might as well have walked about town wearing a sandwich board which said 'loser' both front and back. None of the girls believed he would amount to anything and they were all planning on marrying someone with a future, someone who would be able to take them away from this small town.

Leroy was just about out of money. If he didn't win this game he'd be out of here. It was his shot. As he lined up what looked like the easiest shot on the table, he heard some of the older guys whooping it up. He stopped to see what the commotion was all about.

"Now there is a fine piece," one of them said.

"Old man, she'd hurt you."

There was lots of laughter and body language being displayed as Leroy stepped to the window. The glass was painted green on the lower half, but all the men were standing and watching a young girl saunter by. Leroy had seen her before but had never been impressed. She seemed very young and a little on the heavy side. Somehow, all the whistles and shouting in the background had the effect of forcing Leroy to take a second look. Not bad, he thought.

As she passed the window where Leroy stood she looked coyly up at him. Leroy winked. The girl smiled.

As he lined up his shot again, he asked if anyone knew who that sweet thing was, but he just heard a lot of laughs for a response.

"You can't handle that, Leroy," his opponent said. "Too much woman for you."

"Put it back in your pants," an older man said. "Give up!"

He missed his first shot. His opponent, after sinking four straight, said, "She's a bit young for you, Leroy. She's still in high school."

Leroy lost, hung up the pool cue and said over his shoulder, "I owe you a beer!", and left.

Three days later, he was standing in front of the school at 3:00 PM. She was nearly the last one out. "Hi, Sugar," Leroy said.

"My name's not 'Sugar'." And she kept walking. She looked kind of sassy, Leroy thought. She had long, dark curly hair that had been left to dry naturally leaving her with a hint of a wild look. Her hair was not the first thing Leroy noticed, however. She was short and just a little pudgy but with a great build. If her waist were an inch or two larger than he would have liked, her breasts were also an inch or two larger than most of the girls, and that he did like. When she spoke to him he was forced to look at her face and he saw sparkling dark eyes which were filled with mischief, a dark but creamy complexion, and a smile that contradicted her words. As he followed her his eyes watched her hips sway in a way he found very sexy. Finally, he caught up to her.

"So what is your name?"

"Bonnie."

"Lots of books you got there," he said. "Want a ride?"

"I don't even know you. I can't take a ride from strangers." She kept walking.

All Bonnie's life, it had been her older sister Marie who guided her, taught her the important things she would need to know, took care of her. Marie was not just a sister, she was a friend.

When Bonnie was fourteen, she worried about boys. She had dated a few times but didn't know what to do when a boy tried to kiss her. She went to Marie, who taught her how to kiss and told her to practice by kissing the back of her own hand.

Several dates later, a boy tried to stick his tongue in Bonnie's mouth. Marie told her that was great! She had already been schooled in keeping her lips moist and parted, knew how to breathe heavily, but Bonnie wondered aloud how to handle a tongue.

"The next time," Marie said, "grab his tongue with your lips and suck."

Bonnie had never heard anything so disgusting but forced herself to try it. The result was amazing. That very same night she had to wake Marie to ask about doing IT. They sat up till the night sky turned grey. Marie's best advice was not to do anything till she had mastered everything Marie had taught her. After all, Bonnie wouldn't get any respect if she didn't do IT right, but if she did... she could have any boy - or man, for that matter - that she wanted.

That same night Marie shared her magazine collection with Bonnie. She told her to read them all, cover to cover.

"You can learn lots from these," Marie said.

They talked about breathing, kissing, hugging, where to put your hands, and finally came down to the two most important things.

"Never, and I mean never, make the first move," Marie said. "It's just like dancing. The guy always leads. Otherwise he won't respect you.

"When he puts his hand under your blouse, then you can do the same. When he unhooks your bra, then you can unbutton his shirt. There's only one exception. When he touches you down there, don't you do anything but start squirming around a little bit and start your heavy breathing. And maybe a little moaning."

"But what if he wants me to touch him?"

"Oh. He will! But don't do it. Make him wait as long as you can."

"Then what? Are we getting to the good part?"

"Nope! Now we're getting to the hard part." Both girls giggled. "Before you can do any of the things I told you, you have to learn muscle control. And you have to practice till you get it right."

"What muscles?" Bonnie said. "Teach me! Show me how!"

"Okay. From now on, every time you go to take a pee, you have to squeeze down with those muscles to shut it off. Right in the middle. And no dripping. When you can do that, then start practicing doing it two or three times in a row. When you can do it all the way through, you know, start... stop... start... stop, then you'll be ready."

For the first few days, every time Bonnie tried this new trick she started to giggle. Finally, on the third day, she came running out of the bathroom after dinner and fairly screamed, "Marie! I did it!." It was unfortunate that both her parents were there and graced her with a puzzled look.

Later, Marie told her to keep practicing and as soon as she could do it quickly three times in a row, she could start practicing doing it even when she wasn't peeing. It wasn't long before Bonnie found herself practicing in the classroom with a smug half smile on her face.

This continued for over an eighteen month period before Marie deemed Bonnie ready. In the meantime, word had spread fast among the boys in school. Bonnie was a tease. Heavy kissing, but that was all. If things got a little out of hand, she would push the enamored boy away and say, "I've got my respect, you know."

Marie had said that now she could have her pick of any boy or man she wanted and she was not taking the selection lightly. She had been 'ready' for nearly two months when she first met Leroy but was still looking over the field.

Three more times she saw Leroy. Once in front of the school and twice at a local restaurant where Leroy occasionally sat drinking coffee. Each time, he said, "Hi Bonnie! Good to see you!" She was thrilled that he remembered her name. She had no idea he was stalking her.

On the fourth occasion, they talked for several minutes and Leroy bought her a donut and some coffee, and he offered to walk her home. He asked her if she wanted to meet him for a beer that night. "I can't do that! I'm only fifteen," she said.

"Jesus H. Christ! Jail bait." He stood looking at her like she was an insect.

"What's that mean?" Bonnie said, her head coyly lowered but her eyes watching his face.

He explained that he was a grown up man and that he couldn't be fooling around with no kid. She had to be at least sixteen or he would end up in jail. She told him in only six weeks she would turn sixteen, and as the tears started, she turned and ran for home.

It was nearly two weeks before she saw him again. This time, he apologized and said maybe he'd take her out for her birthday… make it a big celebration.

She knew he was the one. She began to want him shortly after he explained the concept of jail bait. She began practicing in earnest. Only a month to go.

5.

Bonnie's birthday was on a Friday. He picked her up from school and took her home. In the car, in front of her house, he told her what to wear and that he'd meet her at the coffee shop at seven.

"I can't do that," Bonnie said. "My dad wants to meet all the boys I date."

"Not a good idea. First, I'm not a boy. And that's bound to upset your old man. See, fathers don't like it when their daughters grow up and today's the day you turned sixteen. So you're grown up now. If he sees me, a full grown man, it would just remind him how old you're getting. Nope. Bad idea."

Bonnie could see the logic in that. In fact, wasn't it just yesterday her dad had shouted at her that she wasn't grown up yet? He would keep her a little girl her whole life if she let him. She agreed to meet Leroy at seven. They were going to have dinner and see a movie.

She started with a quick shower so she could shave her legs and her pits. Then she pulled the stopper on the tub and let the shower fill the tub, spraying hot water over her body. While she lay there she practiced her muscle control.

When the water cooled, she stepped out, combed her curly hair and began putting on make-up. Just a little so her dad wouldn't get upset. She would tell him some girlfriends were giving her a birthday party.

She put on fresh, pink panties and a new bra and stood looking at herself in the mirror. She liked what she saw. She had filled out nicely. Finally she pulled a silk blouse off the satin covered hanger and slipped it over her shoulders. Looked in the mirror again. With a mischievous smile, she removed the blouse and the bra, then put the blouse on again. Better. She had borrowed one of Marie's shortest skirts. It was a bit tight through the rear, but boy, did she look great, she thought, pirouetting in front of the mirror. Over the blouse she pulled one of her school sweaters and added a longer skirt, well below her knees. Ready!

She glided down the stairs and floated into the kitchen.

Watched her mother preparing dinner.

"Mom? Some of the girls at school invited me over to have a birthday party for me. Is it okay if I go?" She knew her mother would look like she was considering whether to object but would ultimately give in. As soon as she did, Bonnie said, "What time would you like me to be home?" She asked that way knowing her mother would give her all the slack in the world.

"Darling, you're sixteen and practically grown. You use your best judgement. I'll tell dad we're going to celebrate your birthday tomorrow. That is, if he even remembers today is your birthday." Her mom laughed. "Have a good time and call if you need a ride home."

She was an hour early but if she had waited any longer, she'd have had to face her dad and that could get sticky, so she just quietly waited for Leroy at the coffee shop after using the restroom to shed the sweater and the extra skirt.

She felt like a princess that night. Leroy came with his pickup all cleaned up, inside and out. Instead of his usual Levi's and engineer boots with a stained T-shirt, he was wearing cotton slacks, a dress shirt with a tie not quite pulled up all the way, dress cowboy boots that had been neatly shined. A sport coat hung over the back of the seat. He had a special place in mind for this celebration, he told her as he pinned a corsage just above her left breast.

They drove about forty miles to a little Italian restaurant. He ordered Chianti with their meal and she giggled when the waiter looked her over but didn't ask for any proof of age. She had never had wine before and it made her pleasantly light headed. The meal was good and Leroy impressed her by paying with a credit card.

They saw a love story at a place that showed six films at once. She had never seen a movie house like this one. And a love story. All her other dates had taken her to see gruesome, violent movies. Leroy was really special.

After the movie, he took her to a motel. She almost bolted, but Leroy reminded her she was a woman now and he had prepared a special evening for them. He told her to wait while he registered. When he returned he drove slowly around the building till they found their room. He opened the truck door for her and pulled a cooler out of the bed of the truck.

"What's in there?" she said.

"The makings of a picnic lunch just for the two of us."

The room was clean and smelled of potpourri. There was a bed, naturally, a small couch, one table, one chair, and a writing desk. Leroy turned on the TV and handed her the remote control, telling her it's her choice. He began pulling out items from his cooler. Two shrimp cocktails, an aluminum tray with cheese and crackers, and a bottle of wine. Special wine, he told her. What he didn't tell her is it was about one third vodka.

After the first drink, he kissed her forehead and said "Happy Birthday". He gave her a silk scarf wrapped in cheap gift wrap, but she liked it. She liked the kiss, too.

Halfway through their second drink, while she was beginning to feel dizzy, Leroy discovered a joint in his jacket pocket. He re-twisted the ends and lit it. She knew about marijuana but had never tried it. He asked if she wanted a hit but she refused. Leroy didn't press it. Instead, after inhaling, he kissed her again, this time on the lips, and slowly. She had been holding her breath, but when he felt her begin to breath through her nose, he exhaled through his nose. She couldn't help but inhale some of the smoke.

"What do you think?" he said.

"It tickled. But it's not bad." He held the smoldering joint toward her lips. She looked at it for a moment, looked at Leroy, then took a small drag and blew the smoke out.

"No, no, no. You have to inhale it!"

She tried again, inhaled, and coughed a little. A few minutes later she thought she had never felt so good.

When she was finally in bed, naked but smiling, she found it almost impossible to remember all the things Marie had taught her. Concentration was difficult but she remembered the muscle control. All that practice.

If nothing else, they found they had at least one thing in common. An extraordinary sex drive.

Leroy had never dreamed it could be like this. All the smut rags he had so avidly read were wrong. This was much better. His previous experience seemed so dismal by comparison he blanked it from his memory. He remained high all night without further need of drugs. He was in love.

6.

Leroy took her home the following morning. It was nearly six. Her father stood in the doorway in his shorts with his beefy arms on his hips glaring at them. Leroy reached across the pickup cab and opened her door.

"I'll call you." Strangely, he meant it.

Bonnie told her dad Leroy was a girlfriend's brother who offered her a ride home, that the party just lasted forever and they had talked themselves to sleep. Luckily the brother had been there to give her a lift.

Whether her dad believed her was questionable. In any case, she was grounded for a month.

Leroy did call. Several times. She only hoped he would wait for her month to pass.

He did wait for the punishment period to pass and they continued to meet two or three times a week for the next several months, but there were no more fancy dinners, movies or motel rooms. They did their grappling on the seat of the pickup but were happy with that arrangement.

On her next birthday, she begged Leroy to meet her family. When he refused, she blurted, "I'm pregnant."

7.

"Pat, yesterday you expressed an interest in criminal law. Is that idle speculation or is that the direction you're planning on taking?"

"I guess I don't know for sure, but it seems the most interesting and probably the most challenging."

"Well, there's a trial beginning next Monday in Bay City. Might be a good idea if we attend. A little exposure wouldn't hurt."

"Monday!? Does that mean…"

"Yep. It does mean."

They left on Sunday with A.J. doing the driving. He couldn't seem to keep up with traffic and Pat was getting antsy just watching the cars flow by. When they reached I-75, A.J. pulled into one of the two service stations near the ramps and announced he needed a pit stop. When he returned, he tossed the keys to Pat. "South, for about an hour." Pat made it in forty two minutes.

"See that next exit… Wilder Road? You'll want to get off there and turn left."

Pat drove through a residential neighborhood that was old but well cared for. There were a couple shopping centers that looked a little run down, a car dealership, some fast food places.

"Getting hungry?" A.J. said.

Pat thought he could do without any food but said, "Nah, but we can stop if you'd like."

After several miles the road curved to the right and they crossed a drawbridge.

"Turn right at the next light."

This neighborhood was even older. There was an automotive factory and a few run-down bars. Pat could see the skyline of the downtown area just ahead and a little to the left.

"You're going to want to make a left... um, I think it's Washington Street. Anyhow, at the light just before the next bridge. Can't miss it."

Pat followed A.J.'s instructions and was now at the edge of the downtown area.

"This next light. Make another left and at the end of that block you'll have to turn right. That's it. Next light make a left again. Now, see this little side street? Whoa! Slow down. This is it. Turn here." Another left. "One more left into this driveway."

"But A.J., that sign says 'No Trespassing'."

"Ignore it. Now cut behind that abandoned building and cut across this lot to the far side. Good! Park anywhere."

"Won't we get a ticket?" Pat said.

They were in an abandoned parking lot which had been taken over partially by a few U.S. Post Office trucks and lots of weeds.

A.J. ignored the question and was getting out of the car. They were walking much the reverse of the way they had driven in. When they got back to Washington Street, A.J. looked up at the old stained federal building. "This is it. Post Office on the ground floor and the court's upstairs.

C'mon. Let's go find a motel."

Monday found them seated near the back of the courtroom listening to two attorneys argue about the wording in a contract. The judge had asked for briefs to be filed and was adjourning. He looked out over his courtroom and his gaze settled for a moment on A.J. and Pat.

"A.J.! Is that you?" the judge said.

A.J. smiled a response.

"Would you be kind enough to approach?" To the U.S. Marshall standing at ease to the side, he said, "Please clear the courtroom."

"A.J.! You old son of a bitch," the judge said. "I thought you'd be dead by now. How the hell are you?"

"Well, I'm able to sit up and take nourishment, as they say. And you?"

"I'm fine... just fine. So, why are you in my courtroom on a nice sunny day like this? You're not checking up on me, are you?"

"Nope! But I do have a motive. That young man I was sitting with is my great grandson. He's interested in the great paper chase. Thought I'd expose him to the Capital Crimes case being heard today. Who's presiding?"

"Why, I am. Along with Charlie Brewster and Sandra Kowalski. Why don't we go into my chambers. I believe there's fresh coffee." Turning to the Marshall he shouted, "Hey, Hank!" Then he returned his attention to A.J. "What's the boy's name?"

"Pat. Pat Ripplestone."

"Hell's fire! That's no name for a lawyer." He turned again toward Hank. "Bring the boy... um, Pat Ripplestone, to my chambers please."

As he left the bench he was already removing his robe.

Beneath it he wore a revolver in a shoulder holster.

"Do you really need that?" A.J. said.

"Nah. I just enjoy the hell out of it. How do you take your coffee? Cream? Sugar? Or maybe just a little poison?"

The judge poured two coffees and added a finger of brandy to his own and two fingers to A.J.'s. When Pat came in he got his with cream and sugar. A.J. introduced Pat and promptly forgot he was in the room. The two old barristers went back a lot of years and hadn't seen each other in some time. Lots of catching up to do, but they spent the time verbally sparring and enjoying it immensely. Pat was amused and in awe of the elderly gentlemen at the same time.

The clerk came in and announced the courtroom was ready.

The judge asked if Brewster and Kowalski were ready, as well. The clerk confirmed that they were, so the judge rose, put on his robe and headed into the hall where the other two judges were walking toward them. They spent only a few minutes greeting A.J. then moved toward the door leading into the courtroom.

At the last moment the judge turned to Pat and winked at him. "You may enjoy this, son."

Pat heard someone shout, "All rise!" as the door closed behind the trio. A.J. grabbed Pat's elbow and led him away.

"Damn. We'll have to walk halfway around the building and go through the metal detectors again. Hope there's still decent seating left." A.J. continued to grumble under his breath as they made their way around the ancient but well cared for building.

Pat liked this old building. It was regal. Not like the modern court buildings in California. This was like from an old movie. It had class. It even smelled like… well, like a court house.

They passed security again and made their way to the courtroom. There was another Marshall standing guard at the doors. "Sorry. Court's in session." A.J. was turning crimson above his collar, but hadn't said anything yet. "Wait," the guard said. "Are you Judge Ripplestone?"

"My name's Ripplestone."

"Please go in, your honor. You've been cleared."

"Thank God for friends in high places," A.J. mumbled as they quietly made their way down the aisle.

There were three judges on the bench. The one in the middle, A.J.'s friend, was introducing the other judges and presenting the rules of his courtroom. The attorneys, who had obviously heard this before, seemed to be ignoring him and were shuffling their papers. There were only two attorneys present, a young heavy woman who looked a little dazed, the recorder, the clerk, and the same Marshall who had led Pat to the judge's chambers.

Pat was fascinated by the decor. Portraits of long dead judges hung high on the walls. The windows had to be fifteen feet high, there was ancient oak everywhere. The judge said, "Counselor for the defense, you may begin. You have six hours for your presentation. Does the accused speak for herself?"

The defense attorney slowly rose to his feet. "No, your honor. I will speak for the defense."

The judge gazed down at the young woman. "Do you agree to allow counsel to speak on your behalf?"

The young woman, still seated, nodded affirmatively.

"Please stand when addressing the court. And speak clearly. The recorder cannot hear that you were nodding!"

The woman's chair made a scraping sound on the polished oak floor as she stood. "Y-yessir, your honor, sir." She remained standing.

"You may be seated. Counselor, begin."

8.

Leroy agreed to meet her family with more than a little reluctance, and in the interest of putting it off as long as possible, claimed he would be out of town till the next weekend.

Two days later, shortly after midnight, there was a sad tapping on Leroy's front door. His mother answered. "Bonnie! What are you doing here?"

Bonnie's face was tear stained. Her clothing was disheveled. She carried a gym bag that had not been completely zipped and several garments spilled out. The bag had 'Tigers' written across the side in the famous Detroit Tigers script. Leroy's mother quickly grabbed her and pulled her into the room and half hugged her.

"What happened? Are you hurt? Oh, Bonnie! You look terrible. Who did this to you?"

Bonnie couldn't answer. She began crying in earnest again. The sobs turned into violent hiccups. When she looked up from the comforting shoulder, Bonnie could see Leroy in the hall. He had no shirt or socks on. Just his dirty Levi's. The expression on his face was unreadable. Did he want her to leave? To just disappear? The tears began again.

It was nearly ten minutes before she could speak, then she blurted out, "I'm kicked out!" The short sentence ended in another soft wail. Her shoulders were still racked with heavy sobs.

Slowly the story came out. Her dad had found out about the pregnancy. It occurred to Bonnie that this was not the way she wanted her future mother-in-law to discover that she would soon be a grandmother, but the words were out before she could stop herself. She looked up at the woman who had been comforting her and tried to apologize but no words came. But it seemed to be all right. The woman continued to hug her and made soft and comforting cooing noises.

By morning, the entire story was clear. Her dad was livid with rage and before physically throwing Bonnie from the porch had hit her mother several times, as well. She had no place to go, wasn't married and was pregnant. Bonnie, at that moment, just wanted to die, and said so.

"Nonsense! You'll move in here. It will seem better after you've rested a bit. I'll talk to your father. We'll get it straight. Now why don't you get a nice hot bath and then get some sleep." She took Bonnie and led her down the hall, still making those peculiar cooing noises.

Bonnie was embarrassed to get out of the tub. She realized while lying there that she didn't know Leroy's mother's name. And she was carrying his child! What if he denied it? Should she get an abortion? Her mind was swirling with questions and indecision when Leroy's mom came in.

"Now, I don't want you calling me Mrs. White. You just call me Sandy. Or Mom, if you'd be more comfortable with that. All the kids Leroy grew up with always called me 'Mom', so I'm used to it. Brought you a robe and here's a nice terry cloth towel. Robe might not fit but it's nice and toasty warm."

Bonnie could hear Leroy and Sandy talking distantly through the walls but couldn't make out the words at all. She could just imagine Leroy denying everything. Her last thought before drifting into a troubled sleep was that she wished she were dead.

The next day, she awoke to a silent house. She wandered through the small but clean place and saw evidence that someone had slept on the couch. She wondered briefly if she had taken Sandy's bed or Leroy's. Must have been Sandy's. Smelled too good to be Leroy's.

On the small kitchen table, there was a note... 'Please stay. Went to the store for a few things. Be back, SW'

The request to stay nearly made her bolt for the door.

She looked around for her clothes with a little panic in her eyes but it was too late. The front door was opening.

"Well, good morning, Sunshine. You're looking lots better. Let me look at you." Sandy held her at arm's length and looked her over with a practiced mother's eye. "I think you'll be fine. Have you seen a doctor, yet?"

By the end of that week she not only looked better, but felt better, too. Leroy had proposed - without any coercion - and Sandy insisted on an engagement party, and best of all, Leroy seemed real happy about being a father.

They were definitely going to keep the baby. They had made some plans for a marriage. Sandy would drive with them to Las Vegas. They would be married there with Sandy as the witness, then they would honeymoon there. Leroy said he knew he could get a decent job and things would work out fine. Sandy encouraged them to head straight for Detroit. That's where the really good jobs were. Get into Ford or General Motors, she advised. Big pay and benefits, too. After all, she told them, they would need health insurance with a baby on the way.

Sandy left them in Las Vegas twenty minutes after the ceremony. She had stuffed a wrinkled envelope in Bonnie's hand as she kissed her good-bye. It contained a wedding card and three hundred dollars.

Leroy and Bonnie calculated that it would take about one hundred of those dollars to get them to Detroit. They spent the rest on their honeymoon. They didn't gamble and the only shows they saw were at a couple of bars well away from the strip. They stayed in the least expensive room they could find and ran out of money in only five days. But they had seen the lights, felt the atmosphere and wandered through the big name casinos, just looking. The night they left, they each put three dollars into a slot machine, but there was no payoff. Although a hostess did get them free drinks. Leroy tipped the girl a dollar.

"Thanks, Shooter," the waitress said.

When they arrived in Detroit they had only seven dollars left and a few coins. They hadn't thought about where they would stay. Up till now, they slept in the pickup, cuddled together. The trip had taken three days and by now they both needed a shower. Bonnie was miserable and began wondering if this had all been a mistake. That night they slept on the side of I-94, a dangerous thing to do, but they survived.

The next morning, Leroy washed as best he could in the men's room of a Shell station and they drove straight to the General Motors Cadillac Stamping Plant on Connors at I-94. Nothing. They tried three more plants without any luck and ran out of gas near Seven Mile and John R. Not one of Detroit's finer neighborhoods.

The next morning, they split the money they had left.

Leroy left on foot, vowing that he would have a job before the day was out. As he left, Bonnie was crying. "And what if you don't?" was the last thing Leroy heard her say.

Shortly after noon, Leroy stopped in a coffee shop and spent the last of his money on a ham and cheese sandwich which he washed down with water. He sat on a stool at the bar rather than at a table. The guy next to him insisted on a continuing string of conversation. Finally, Leroy, beside himself with his problems, lashed out at the elderly man. But it turned out to be the best thing he had done all day. After hearing the young fellow's story, the old man pointed down the road.

"Walk that way," the old man said. "You'll come across a block building painted yellow. You'll have to kick on the door, and don't give up. They're in there. They just won't open up if you knock like some gentleman. They'll give you a job and pay cash, too. Hard work, but they pay every night before you leave. Skinny as you are, though, you'll have to do some powerful convincing to get that job."

The old man left and Leroy fingered the money in his pocket. Thirteen cents. He walked back into the cafe and left his last thirteen cents as a tip.

He found the yellow building with no trouble. It was bright yellow. There were scuff marks on the door where others had kicked the news of their arrival. There were two windows filled with glass block and there were several bullet holes in each.

Leroy tried the door. Locked. He knocked four times, using the flat of his hand. Nothing. He looked up and down the street. No one seemed to be paying any attention to him, so he kicked the door twice, as hard as he could. All the frustration he had bottled up inside was suddenly spent on that door. He was about to kick again, this time intending to break the door down, when it suddenly opened. A grizzled old man appeared, not much bigger than Leroy.

"Yeah? What the hell you want? And quit your gosh dammit kicking!!" The old man had long white hair, tinted yellow. The side of his face was nicotine stained from the cigarette he apparently habitually held in the corner of his mouth. His clothes were unbelievably dirty. His boots had years of black crud hanging from them. There was a gap between his yellowed teeth and he hadn't shaved in better than a week. And he held a gun.

Leroy's eyes were fixed on the gun. It was held casually, as if the old man knew he wouldn't need it. Over the old man's left shoulder Leroy could see a young woman standing in a doorway. She looked wary and kept her eyes on the old man's head.

"I want to see the owner." Leroy had practically shouted the request.

"He ain't here. Come back later." And the old man was trying to close the door.

Leroy, even in the face of the gun, pushed the door open and burst inside. "I need to see him now. I need a job and 'later' ain't good enough. I need a job now!"

He was sweating, his eyes bulged, and he had meant every word. He'd rather take his chances on getting killed than leave without a job.

The old man, who had raised the gun to Leroy's chest, stepped back, looked Leroy over very slowly, and said to the girl in the doorway, "Get Clem." He continued to study Leroy while the girl dropped something heavy and metallic on a desk inside the room she was in.

"Job, huh? You don't look like you can handle much of a job, sonny!" One bloodshot eye closed and he said, "Can you lift a hundred pounds in each of those skinny arms then throw it a good ten feet? Could you do that? All day long? Huh?" He looked at Leroy's boots. "Damnable sissy."

Clem sauntered in wiping grease from work hardened hands. "What do you want, Pa?"

"Kid says he needs, and I mean NEEDS, a job."

Clem wasn't much older than Leroy but looked much tougher. He was dirty, but under the grime his clothes were expensive work clothes. Made to last. He looked up at Leroy and with the briefest of glances knew the need was real. "What do you do? I mean, what kind of job you looking for?"

Clem was already walking away. They cut through the room the young girl was in. It was a small office. Dirt permeated the place. The floor, tiled, was thick with grease. Her desk was old, battered and cluttered. A large revolver caught Leroy's eye.

"Don't mind the guns," Clem said. "This ain't the best neighborhood around. You carrying?" One of Clem's eyebrows rose with the question. "If you are, it goes in the safe right over there when you come in. You don't get it back till it's time to quit."

Clem kicked open a plywood door leading into an outdoor area cluttered with more tires than Leroy had ever seen in one place. There were several trucks parked around the small yard.

"I pay piece-work. It's fair. Penny and a half per tire. See that machine over there? She can do twenty three hundred tires an hour and shreds each one of them into two inch strips. Course, nobody can feed her that fast. But if you could, that's a pretty piece of change in your pocket. No taxes... no benefits. Just cash money. Every day. You still interested?"

Leroy was amazed at what he saw. Four black men were tossing tires onto a conveyor which made its way toward the machine Clem had pointed out. "Sure! When can I start?"

"Right now. And tell you what I'll do. You work hard enough that none of these other guys bitch about you, I'll pay you full share for today's work." Clem showed Leroy to the back of a semi trailer in which two guys were throwing tires out the back and one older man was trying to keep up with the flow. "This is Butch. Give him a hand."

For the next ten hours, without a break, Leroy caught bouncing, rolling tires, filled with water, mud, and stones, and half rolled, bounced and threw them on the conveyor.

Finally, Clem climbed over a stack of oversized tires and hit the stop button, bringing the machinery and the conveyors to a halt. The men gathered close. Clem pulled out a wad of cash from his coverall pocket.

Without looking up he asked, "Anyone got anything to say about the new guy?"

No one responded. Clem glanced at a counter on the front of the machine control panel and gazed to the sky, mentally calculating the pay for each of the men. He paid Leroy last. In cash. One hundred forty four dollars and thirty cents. Leroy didn't know if it was correct or not and didn't care.

"You gonna be back tomorrow?" Clem said.

"You bet."

"Okay. We start at six on the day shift and generally work ten hours, sometimes longer. Depends on how many tires come in. We're closed Sundays. Be here about ten minutes early and I'll introduce you around." Leroy had a career.

Bonnie screamed when he opened the pick up door. Then she started crying. Leroy put his arm around her and tried to calm her. "You're all wet", she said, still blubbering. "And you stink." She tried to push him away.

Leroy pulled out his pay and waved it in front of her.

"This don't stink. C'mon. Let's go find a motel, get a shower, some food and some sleep."

They walked down to Seven Mile Road to catch a bus and Bonnie pestered him with questions all the way to the intersection. They passed his employer's yard and Leroy boasted about his new job, the impressive machinery, how much a tire weighed and how many tires he threw that day.

They didn't notice the looks they drew walking after dark in perhaps one of the worst neighborhoods Detroit had to offer. The only thing that gave them safe passage was they looked as though they hadn't a penny between them. And until recently, that was the truth.

The bus driver looked at them with clear distaste and when Leroy asked to be taken to the nearest motel, the bus driver said, "This ain't no damn taxi."

Only six stops down Leroy spotted a motel with a vacancy sign. They got off the bus at the next stop and walked the four blocks to the run down motel. It was boarded up. Two more blocks brought them to a motel with a neon sign that read, "Rest Awhile! Low rates. Clean Rooms. Cable -V" The "T" had been broken. They had to pay in advance.

The television didn't work but the shower did and Leroy washed with his clothes on and when he was halfway clean Bonnie joined him. He was too tired to go out to eat, and the motel didn't have a restaurant, but the guest card in the room listed a pizza place that delivered. They bought a large with four beers.

The next morning, Leroy gave all but twenty dollars to Bonnie, asked her to get some gas in the truck and bring it to the motel. He would be back by five that afternoon. If she had enough money, she should get them some food to eat in the room and maybe look for a little better motel. Or maybe an apartment. She should ask the desk clerk for a decent neighborhood within a few miles of work. They faced this new day with more enthusiasm than any since they had married.

9.

They found a house to rent, although it wasn't much of a house, but they reasoned they would be able to save enough to move to a nicer place in a better neighborhood within a year or two.

Leroy's job was paying well and things were looking up.

He had been given more responsibility at work and after six months found there were only two people there who had more seniority than he. He took pride in throwing more tires than anyone else and was especially pleased when he was called upon to work on the equipment whenever it broke down. On those occasions Clem paid him twelve bucks an hour while the other workers got no pay until the machine began eating tires again.

From Bonnie's point of view, there were only a few things that spoiled the perfect marriage.

Shortly after they had found the house they were living in, Leroy was rolled on his way home from work. She was scared half to death. He had lost nearly two hundred dollars but she didn't care about that. His lip was torn and swollen and he had a big knot on the back of his head. That alone was scary but what really bothered her is that two days later he came home with a pistol. She knew guns cost a lot more than the fifty dollars he had paid for it, so she believed the gun was hot and had probably been used in a crime somewhere, but she couldn't talk Leroy out of carrying it.

As the pregnancy continued, she gained nearly forty pounds and she could tell by the look on Leroy's face that he didn't like that. He never said anything but she knew how he felt about fat women from the way he made fun of them at the supermarket. She couldn't decide if this is what caused her depression or merely added to it. She wished she had someone close she could talk to.

She even thought Leroy sometimes was not working when he would come home late. She tried to match the money he brought home with the hours he had been gone but he kept telling her that he was paid piecework and the pay didn't relate to the time spent away from home.

Her suspicions made her even more miserable.

Perhaps the worst thing was their sex life. As she gained weight Leroy didn't respond to her advances as he had before. Even though he re-assured her sex was bad for the baby she was convinced it was her weight. During the last six weeks of the pregnancy Leroy insisted on masturbation if she felt any desires she couldn't control. She felt completely unfulfilled on those occasions and invariably felt so testy the next morning they would have a fight. After Leroy left for work she wanted to apologize, but by then it was always too late.

They had no pre-natal care. When the baby was nearly due, they discovered that without insurance they would have to pay the hospital in cash before she would even be admitted. Leroy groused about losing all the savings they had accumulated and Bonnie felt a little more worthless when he said such things.

She figured five hundred dollars would be enough and she began carrying that amount in the bottom of her purse, wrapped in an old handkerchief.

Finally, the baby arrived. She called Leroy at work and he rushed home and drove like a mad man to the hospital where they discovered their five hundred dollars was two thousand less than the admitting fee.

Leroy called Clem and he promised to bring the cash as quickly as he could get there. In the meantime, just as Leroy thought of pulling his gun to convince the stubborn nurse to let Bonnie in, Bonnie fainted and two orderlies swept her onto a gurney and disappeared down the hall, leaving Leroy to continue negotiating with the admitting nurse. Finally, Clem arrived.

It was a girl.

The early joy they felt was soon overcome by their continuing troubles. Leroy began working late again and began telling Bonnie to exercise if she expected to lose any weight. She reacted by hugging her baby and eating to make herself feel better. The pounds continued to accumulate and their sex life was practically non-existent.

One night it was too hot to sleep with the windows closed and thinking Leroy would be home soon, Bonnie took the baby to bed with her and left the doors and windows unlocked and wide open. She heard the floor in the bedroom creak and looked toward the digital clock on the cardboard nightstand.

She felt a gloved fist plow into her cheek and eye and instinctively rolled over to protect her baby, thinking that Leroy was drunk. But it wasn't Leroy. The intruder rummaged through the drawers in the bedroom and then went into the living room. She didn't know what he was doing but could hear noises for what seemed an eternity but was determined not to cry out herself.

Even after the intruder left, she remained in the bed cowering over her baby.

Finally Leroy came home, turned on the lights and saw the damage that had been done. He rushed into the bedroom to find his wife and child on the floor in the corner, his wife terrified.

The next day he brought home another gun. This one smaller. A woman's gun, he told her.

Bonnie lived in fear. She begged him not to go to work, or at least, to come home while it was still daylight, but Leroy insisted they needed the money before they could move to a better neighborhood. Every night, Bonnie sat on the floor of the bedroom holding her baby in one arm and holding the gun in her other hand, waiting for Leroy to return.

Less than two weeks later, the intruder returned. She fired but missed. He kicked her solidly. The gun went skittering beneath the bed. In a semi-conscious state she moved to protect the baby. The intruder dove to the floor and recovered the weapon. As he jumped back to his feet and swung the weapon to point at her, she screamed and raised one hand as if to ward off any bullets while pulling her screaming child to her bosom.

The intruder mistook her flailing arm as a second attack and fired at the shape on the floor, killing the baby. He turned and ran from the room, dropping the gun as he careened off the door jamb.

Bonnie picked up the gun and pointed it at the retreating shadow but didn't fire. She turned to the baby and realized that she was bloody.

When Leroy returned from work, he found his wife in a state of shock on the bedroom floor with both arms around the baby and the gun in her left hand. With the living room light on and the bedroom still darkened, all she could see was his silhouette.

Suddenly Bonnie screamed, raised the gun and fired once, killing Leroy.

For some time she remained in the corner, huddled on the floor and then she began screaming. The screams continued for so long and with such a depth of feeling, a neighbor finally called the police. Not because they were worried about Bonnie, but because she had been disturbing their sleep.

10.

The young defense attorney spoke softly and clearly for nearly two hours without interruption, describing Bonnie's early life in a small southern town, crime free and innocent. He was setting a background—a mood.

Pat looked toward the prosecution table and could see the prosecutor was tiring of the defense's discourse and half expected an objection, but there was none forthcoming.

"A.J., what's going on? Why isn't he calling witnesses?

And where's the jury?" Pat said in the lowest whisper he could manage.

"It's almost lunch. I'll explain it then." A.J. said, patting Pat's knee.

The defense attorney had just described Leroy and Bonnie driving away from Las Vegas in a ten year old truck with bad tires, minimal insurance, and only one hundred dollars to their names. The judge said, "Excuse me, counselor. Would this be an opportune time for a recess?"

"Yes sir. This would be an ideal spot for a break," the attorney said.

"Good. And can you give us an approximation of how much time you'll likely need to conclude?"

"About three hours, your honor."

"Very well. This court stands in recess. All parties to be present and prepared to continue at... "the judge looked at the large clock at the back of the courtroom. "Shall we say one o'clock?"

No one responded so the judge rapped his gavel and the three judges, both attorneys and the heavy girl all stood.

"C'mon," A.J. said, "before we get stuck kibitzing with the judge. I'm buying."

11.

They ate at a small diner across the street from the federal building. As they entered, the prosecutor, seated at a corner table with three associates Pat didn't notice in the courtroom, saw A.J. and waved. A.J. nodded in return but did not speak to the man as they passed his table.

A little farther toward the rear sat the defending attorney, also with several strangers. There was no recognition in the young attorney's eyes as he looked at A.J. when they passed.

They selected a corner table at the back of the restaurant and Pat looked around the room, crowded with men in suits and several waitresses bustling about.

It was a dive, in Pat's opinion. The chairs were worn and spotted with dried food, the floor was littered with crumbs and empty sugar packets. The walls had a gaudy wall paper covering the upper half while the lower was done in a cheap paneling which was all coated with a layer of dusty grease. He inspected his silverware and began wiping the spoon on the paper napkin provided.

A.J. looked around, not at the decor, but at the other patrons and nodded to several of them.

"Don't worry," A.J. said. "Place doesn't look like much but the food's good. You won't get sick eating here." He smiled as if he could read Pat's thoughts.

When the waitress came by they hadn't looked at the menus yet but A.J. ordered as if he were a regular. Pat ordered the same thing.

As soon as the waitress left, A.J. said, "Well, what do you think so far?"

"So far, I'm pretty confused. We have three judges instead of one, no jury, no witnesses, no conflict between the lawyers, and the defense lawyer is chewing up his allotted time telling stories instead of presenting any facts."

"I thought so," A.J. said. "Never seen a capital crimes case before, have you?"

Pat's answer was to simply lift his shoulders and raise his hands slightly, palms up, with a quizzical look in his eyes.

"The whole story is too long for the time we have right now, but here's the short version. Capital crimes, which carries its own peculiar definition, requires that the case be heard in a federal court by specially qualified judges, a panel of three. Witnesses are not allowed, except under very unusual circumstances, and a jury will never hear one of these cases. The defendant may speak or may be represented and in either case, the testimony is called soft. It's typically told in story fashion, chronologically. Whichever party is speaking, the floor is his and only under exceptional circumstance may the opponent interrupt. The panel of judges determine a fixed amount of time for the parties to speak based upon their understanding of the complexity of the case, which is based on briefs filed with the court several weeks in advance. Typically, the time allowed is one day or less for each side. Then the panel of judges retire for consideration and the court re-convenes to hear their judgement. Entire case rarely takes over three days. The prosecutor is a federally employed attorney who has special qualifications and the defense attorney, although he also has special qualifications, is selected from the general availability of attorneys at the time the case becomes available. They are each paid according to a federally controlled scale which is typically about half what they would get for a non-capital case. Questions?"

"This is nuts," Pat said. "A capital case... Well, you would think that a capital case deserves the best efforts of all parties, not some scaled down version of justice."

"Hmmm. Maybe. That's still pretty controversial. But there's a reason for everything. Imagine that the accused has millions and millions of dollars he's willing to spend to get acquitted. Would he get the same level of justice as some poor schmuck... Well, never mind. I'm about to get into the long version. We'll save that for the ride home and maybe the next few nights on the porch. In the meantime, this system is as fair as any we've come up with. Just keep watching and listening. You're about to witness the niche of the law that I've spent nearly my entire career involved with. Perhaps it will be clearer as things progress. Now, let's get back. Don't want to rile old friends in the legal system. I may have to stand before this panel again someday."

A.J. left a wad of bills on the table and they walked back across the street. "Told you lunch would be good." A.J. was smiling and humming as they crossed in the middle of the block.

12.

Only a few minutes after A.J. and Pat had returned to their seats the clerk shouted, "All rise." Court was again in session.

The head judge gave a ten minute synopsis of the events of the morning and asked the defense attorney if he were prepared to proceed.

"Yes, your honor," the attorney said.

The young man approached the lectern and took his time opening his notes. He looked up and waited two heartbeats to ensure the panel of judges had given him their attention.

"If it please the court," he began, "we have heard testimony regarding the early life of the defendant up to the point when she and her husband arrived in Michigan. We now will cover the circumstances leading toward the accidental deaths of her husband and infant child."

All three judges raised one eyebrow in unison. Surely the prosecutor would object, thought Pat. But there was no interruption. The defense attorney continued without missing a beat.

Pat was able to listen to the entire presentation with interest. When the attorney described their arrival in Detroit, Pat was appalled at their naiveté. When he heard of their success in finding work and a home he rejoiced on their behalf. When Leroy belittled his wife for her weight gain, he felt a deep sympathy for her and unreasonable anger with Leroy. He celebrated the birth of their child and hoped that event would bring them closer together. He suffered the fears Bonnie must have felt living in her new neighborhood, was aghast at the stories of neighbors ignoring the shots but complaining about her screams because the noise kept them awake.

When that day's session was finished, all persons in the courtroom rose to their feet as the panel of judges left the bench and with the exception of Pat, all turned in unison to leave the courtroom. A.J. had to pull Pat toward the doors.

As they walked out into the late afternoon sun, A.J. said, "Well, what do you think so far?"

Pat was unable to answer immediately and A.J. did not press for an answer. When they reached the car, A.J. said. "I'll drive."

Pat wordlessly got into the passenger side.

A.J. pulled into the parking lot of a quiet neighborhood bar and led the way through the rear door. They sat at a small table along the side wall. As they passed the bar, A.J. ordered a vodka and a scotch, both on the rocks and both with a twist. They sat in silence for some time, A.J. waiting for Pat to finally answer his question.

13.

"How can this be happening? She's completely innocent," Pat said.

"Keep an open mind, boy. You haven't heard the other side of the story."

"It's Pat, not boy," Pat said.

"It's boy and will remain so if you insist on behaving like one," A.J. said.

Pat looked up and saw that A.J. looked displeased.

"Okay, so maybe I'm over-reacting," Pat said. "And you're right, of course. I'll probably swing the other way tomorrow." He offered a sheepish grin in the way of an apology.

"I don't give a damn what you think of the guilt or innocence of that young girl. The point is, you're here to learn something about the way the law works. Now tell me what you saw today."

Pat hoped to recover some of the standing he'd had with A.J. prior to the afternoon session and did his best to reflect on the trial before answering. Finally he had to admit that there was virtually nothing he recognized given his limited exposure to court proceedings, including what he may have read about or seen in movies. He was as confused as he had been earlier, at lunch.

"Nothing to be ashamed about, Pat. It's a new kind of law. It doesn't fit in with any other type of law being practiced today and has very little precedence. The capital crimes legal system was invented a mere forty years ago, give or take a few years, and the implementation has been slow. That's been further compounded by an aura of secrecy. Not that there's anything secret about it. We've just done our best to eliminate press coverage and we've been successful in that regard.

"Now, I've said I'll tell you the long story later. For now let's limit ourselves to specific questions you may have and I'll try to answer them. Go ahead and ask away."

"Okay," Pat said. "First, why is there no jury?"

"We came to the belief that there was no such thing as a jury of your peers. You've heard one side of this woman's story. Do you think you could find fifteen or so jurors who had a background similar to hers and at the same time would not be automatically swayed in her direction? Juries are swayed by emotion, not facts. So we eliminated the jury."

"What about the presentation?" Pat said. "Even I recognized lots of places where an objection seemed appropriate. Yet there were none."

"Objections and rulings on objections are nearly always for the benefit of a jury. A jury doesn't know the law and both attorneys and the judge have a responsibility to disallow information or presentations that may unduly sway jurors. Without a jury present, there is no need for objections. Surely you would agree that the panel of judges know the law well enough to be able to ignore those statements you thought would be objectionable."

"Yeah, I suppose," Pat said.

"There's also two other considerations. If objections were allowed, that automatically would bring in a certain amount of showmanship, which would mean time wasted. We wanted to exclude that, as well. Also, if there should happen to arise, a situation which clearly muddies the waters in a legal sense, either attorney or any of the judges will call for a side bar to discuss the offending issue. Should that happen, the clock stops until the matter is resolved. Don't expect to see a side bar, though. It's generally looked upon as bad form. If there are issues to discuss, they will be handled in chambers after the prosecution has stated his case and before the panel of judges begins deliberations. Anything else?"

"Probably. But I'll wait till after the prosecution presents its case."

"Good," A.J. said. "I'm ready for some dinner and a good night's sleep."

They drained their drinks and left.

"There is one more thing," Pat said.

"What's that?"

"You keep referring to 'we'. Who, exactly, makes up 'we' and how did they get to make the rules?"

A.J. smiled. "That's part of the long story. All in good time, Pat. All in good time."

14.

"All rise. This court is now in session," the clerk said.

For a few minutes there was the subdued noise of spectators seating themselves, the attorneys shuffling papers and the judges making themselves comfortable.

Pat gazed curiously at the defendant. She looked more composed today. Perhaps she felt as though her attorney had made her case well.

"Are the people prepared to begin?" the judge said.

Standing, the prosecutor replied. "Yes sir."

The judges each glanced at the clock. "Please begin."

"If it please the court," the prosecutor began, "the people submit, a sad story not withstanding, the facts will show that the defendant did intentionally and with premeditation, shoot and thus kill her husband, one Leroy White, and did shoot and thus kill her daughter, one…"

The bang of the gavel stilled the prosecutor's presentation but did nothing to quiet the defendant's loud bawling.

"Counselor, control your client or risk having her removed from these proceedings."

The defense attorney was half on his feet, answering the court and at the same time was reaching toward his client, consoling her.

The judge waited a moment for the noise to subside then instructed the prosecutor to continue.

"Ahem." The prosecutor cleared his throat and looked meaningfully at the defendant. "If it please the court." Another long pause while the prosecutor consulted his notes. "The people intend to use substantially less time than is allotted for presentation. A series of facts which we shall present will be conclusive in determining the outcome of this case. The first among these we wish to enter into evidence as exhibit zero, zero, one. A forensic report showing the bullets removed from the victims were fired from the same weapon, a twenty two caliber pistol. This same pistol was found at the scene as described in this police report dated…"

The prosecutor droned on in a bored voice, presenting fact after fact. The bullets came from a specific weapon. That weapon was found at the scene of the crime. Only the defendant's finger prints were discovered on the weapon. The defendant's claim that her husband had given her the weapon for self protection and that he had acquired the weapon from his employer had been denied by the alleged employer. The alleged employer also denied being the husband's employer. Yet the couple were able to pay their rent and purchase food without any visible means of support.

It seemed to Pat to be an excessive amount of evidence and he wondered why the defense attorney had no contradicting evidence. And if there had been statements from witnesses, why couldn't they be cross examined?

"And finally," the prosecutor said, "there had been several months of seemingly unrelated crimes in nearby neighborhoods in which a masked woman, but otherwise matching the defendant's general physical description and bearing, had held up, at gunpoint, several stores. That woman used a twenty two caliber pistol, as well, and in fact, shot a store clerk, killing him. A forensic bullet analysis shows the round from that pistol matches the rounds fired in this instance. We therefore submit, the crime under consideration by this panel is not an accident but part of a pattern of a predator. A woman who is accustomed to using violence to achieve her wants and her needs. Couple these facts with the stirring story the defendant has provided, including the loss of romance in her marriage, caused by the arrival of a baby, and we have a cold blooded murderer who chose to eliminate her problems through violence.

"The people rest."

15.

That afternoon Pat and A.J. met with the prosecutor.

His name was Ted Phillips. He had been a prosecutor for ten years when the Federal Capital Crimes Legal Commission approached him with an offer to consider prosecuting, on the basis of a lifetime commitment, on their behalf. He had accepted.

A.J. introduced Pat as a first year law student anxious to determine his career path and suggested that perhaps Ted would be willing to describe his role in the legal system.

The first thing Pat noticed was a demeanor much different than what he had witnessed in the court room. Ted Phillips behaved more like one of the drier professors Pat had had in California. He was prone to lecturing rather than talking. Ted was a tall man but he slouched much like some of Pat's professors, and he wore half glasses leaving the impression that he was more a scholar than an attorney.

As it turned out, this was closer to the truth than Pat could have known.

A.J. interrupted Ted after only a few minutes and suggested they begin with educational requirements and to make the story brief but chronological.

Ted nodded his assent and began with graduation from law school the first time. "As you undoubtedly know," Ted began, peering intently at Pat over his half glasses, "An attorney begins his career with a degree called juris doctorate. That is frequently mistaken for a true doctorate degree similar to that earned by medical doctors, dentists, philosophers, and the like. But it's not. It's merely a glorified bachelor's degree, in my opinion. If one chooses, one could continue his education and earn a master's degree in any number of specialties of the law. There are damn few lawyers who make that attempt. I, for example, was quite content with my JD.

"I passed the bar on my second try and was already working for the district attorney. I was aware of the Commission—that is, the Capital Crimes Commission—but it never occurred to me that I would ever be involved in that issue, although I was curious as to why an out of town prosecutor always handled those cases.

"When I had accumulated ten years experience, as I said earlier, I was approached by the Commission. I've never come to terms with why I allowed them to convince me to make a career change but I made that decision and have not regretted it.

"There were extensive interviews with a number of well known attorneys, judges and educators. Apparently they found me acceptable. I resigned my position and accepted an income from the Commission as well as a full scholarship to continue my studies. I have three master's degrees—all required— and a doctorate. The initials are JDCC and they stand for Juris Doctorate, Capital Crimes. Those of us who have completed such course work are expected to pass a federal bar exam, and once that is completed, we are licensed to practice anywhere in the country."

"Tell him how long that takes," A.J. said.

"It took me nine years, although there have been some who take longer," Ted said.

"And tell Pat how you earn a living with the weight of all those letters behind your name," A.J. said.

Pat noticed the smallest smirk on A.J.'s face.

"Certainly. I was well received at my old position and in fact, was re-hired at nearly double my old salary. After having passed the federal bar, my Commission pay tripled. I was free to go into private practice if I chose, and whatever my earnings may be, they would not affect my Commission pay. However, and it's a big however, I am required to prosecute any case assigned to me by the Commission within Michigan and by their command, anywhere in the country, as far as that goes."

Seeing the expression on Pat's face, he softened his voice and continued. "But it's not as bad as I'm making it out to be. I practice law privately these days and am only called upon to prosecute capital cases once or twice a year.

"Let me explain how the system works. County prosecutors determine if there is adequate evidence in any case that comes before them. If they choose not to prosecute they are not required to do so, naturally. If a case contains elements of violence, and is a repeat offense, or is a multiple offense, or meets any number of other criteria, and the prosecutor feels there is adequate evidence to proceed, at his option, he may request a review by the Capital Crimes Commission. If the Commission agrees, then the case is moved to the federal level, a defense attorney, who, by the way, has the same academic credentials I have, is assigned, I, or someone like me, is assigned, and we go to trial.

"Now, the specifics of how the trial proceeds is…"

A.J. interrupted Ted once again. "Sorry, Ted," A.J. said, "But we're taking too much of your time and we are about to be late for an appointment. Perhaps we could continue at a future time?"

A.J. was already on his feet and was putting his silver pocket watch away with his left hand while he reached with his right to shake Ted's hand.

As A.J. and Pat walked down the street, Pat asked, "What appointment?"

"It's cocktail time, and I don't think I could have endured another minute of that pompous jerk's rhetoric." A.J. was smiling broadly.

Pat had to agree. "He is boring. But the subject was interesting." Pat walked in silence for a few minutes. "Do you have a doctorate, too?"

"Yep. And he didn't tell you the rest. We all attend at least four credit hours per year to maintain our licenses."

"Are you a Commission prosecutor, too?" Pat said.

"No. I'm an appeals attorney for capital crimes convicts."

"So. Not all the rules have changed," Pat said.

"Well, it's a little different than what you're probably imagining. What happens is, if the defense loses, the defense attorney returns to his normal life and completely forgets about his client. Or, at least tries to. If the defendant feels they were unjustly convicted, they personally can appeal to the Commission. If the Commission feels there may have been an injustice done, they may elect to assign me to that case. I can accept or refuse after having checked the circumstances for myself."

"How many cases do you get a year?" Pat said.

"Oh, in the early years I was fairly swamped. Back then I believed everyone who had a sad tale to tell. I hope I'm just smarter these days and not cynical, but I only find one case every four or five years that merits some attention."

A.J. spoke with a sadness in his voice and an expression that Pat couldn't read.

A.J. changed the subject. "What do you think of your defendant today? Is she still innocent?"

It surprised Pat to discover he had lost track of the defendant. "I don't know. I'm afraid I was more focused on the proceedings than the content. Let me think about it."

They had arrived at the hotel and elected to dine in the hotel dining room and were enjoying a pre-dinner cocktail.

"Well, I think two things," A.J. said. He looked at Pat with a curious expression on his face. "One, I think she's innocent. Two, I think she'll be convicted." A.J. downed his drink and his bearing left no room for a response from Pat.

16.

The following morning found them in court once again.

The judge offered the defense counsel one hour for rebuttal but the attorney for the woman stood and said, "No rebuttal, your honors."

A.J. leaned toward Pat and said, "This is the opportunity for the defense to bring into the court any witness statements or other evidence that would contradict the prosecutor's case. I was afraid there would be none."

The judge spent a few minutes explaining to the defendant that both sides of the case had been heard and that the panel of judges would be retiring to consider the merits of the case. It was anticipated they would use the remainder of that day in deliberations and would reconvene at four o'clock that afternoon. The judge rapped his gavel and everyone stood in unison.

As the young woman turned, Pat saw her face for a moment. She looked exhausted.

A.J. had made an appointment for them to meet with another attorney.

"I think you'll find this gentleman more personable," A.J. said.

They met an elderly gentleman who had retired from all legal work other than Capital cases and he told Pat that, in his opinion, that was one responsibility from which there were no retirees.

Their conversation filled the balance of the morning, continued over lunch served in the gentleman's home, and finally ended about an hour before they were due back in court.

As they drove back to the federal building, A.J. said, "What do you think?"

"He certainly has more genuine compassion than I would have thought a defense attorney under these circumstances might have. He deals with the worst of the worst. How can he continue?"

"Well, there's a couple of things to consider. He's old enough to have been around during the early days when the passion for the new system very nearly destroyed the system. Back then, there was a certain zeal to get the violent criminals out of our civilized society. As a result, there were many who didn't deserve to be tried by the Commission and he's certainly been tainted by that experience. Also, in this type situation, there's not much room for legal tricks and maneuvering. It's just a matter of digging as conscientiously as possible for the truth and then making a clear presentation of things. In that process, the defense attorney can't help but come to some conclusion about his client." A.J. paused for a moment. "I'm sure he does his best regardless of any conclusions he may have reached prior to the verdict."

They had arrived at the federal building.

17.

"This court, having deliberated and having considered all testimony presented, is prepared to announce it's verdict. The defendant will please stand."

There was a shuffling and scraping of chairs as the defense attorney and his client both stood. Bonnie White had twisted a handkerchief into a ball and was gripping it tightly. The attorney had his right arm about her shoulder.

"It is the judgement of this court that the defendant, one Bonnie White, did willfully and with forethought, murder her husband, one Leroy White and did willfully..."

The judges words were drowned out by the wails from the young woman but he didn't stop speaking. She began to slip from her attorney's grasp and slid slowly to the floor. No one made any move to help her.

"...and in consideration of the fact that there were two victims and in consideration of the fact that there had been previous violence attached to the defendant, this court finds the request for punishment according to the rules of the Federal Capital Crimes Legal Commission, Article Seven, Paragraphs Two A and Two B, is within reason and so declares Banishment to be appropriate. This case is closed."

The judge rapped his gavel once, the panel rose, and left the room. Only then did a matron move toward Bonnie White.

There was no celebration at the prosecutor's table. He merely retrieved the note pads in front of him, placed them in a briefcase and turned to leave the building. The defense attorney delayed leaving until Bonnie was out of the courtroom, then he too quietly picked up his notes and left the area.

When Pat and A.J. stood to leave, there was no one left in the room.

18.

A.J. and Pat were seated in A.J.'s hotel room and both were sipping vodka on the rocks. A.J. had his shoes off and sat on the only chair in the room. Pat sprawled across the bed with both pillows behind his back. There was only one light on in the room.

"So what does banishment mean?" Pat said.

"You remember the history of Australia? It was a penal colony. We have one, too. Except it's a man-made island. She'll spend the rest of her life on that island, unless of course, she successfully appeals. And the odds against that are great."

It was quiet in the room and the subdued lighting matched their moods. Both were quiet for some time.

"How's your drink?" A.J. said.

"I'm good."

"Well, I don't usually have more than one a day but I'm in the mood for a second. Do you mind?" A.J. was already on his feet moving to the bottle and ice bucket on the night stand. No answer was expected and none was forthcoming.

"Where is this island?"

"South Pacific," A.J. said. "It's the result of a campaign promise made by some politician years ago. Said he would do something about the state of the nation's landfills. So he managed to get laws passed and various environmental groups to agree, and then we started shipping selected trash out to the new dump site.

"They found a place where there had been earthquake activity and the earth's plates apparently climbed over one another creating a long ridge in the ocean floor. A few years later there developed some underwater volcanic activity and the result was sunken islands just below the surface. It represented a navigation hazard. The garbage piled on those sunken islands made real islands solving the navigation problem, but the cost of transporting trash was a problem. So they wondered how they could make use of the area and eventually turned it into a penal colony."

The story had caught Pat's interest and he was more attentive now. "That's the same as killing those prisoners. You can't expect them to live on a pile of garbage. What about food and water? Did they have to eat old garbage?"

A.J. smiled. "No. Raw garbage was never taken there.

Just inert trash that would eventually return to the soil without contaminating anything. When they decided to use it as a prison, the island was about, oh, a hundred thousand acres, or so, and it was about forty feet above sea level with the highest area about a thousand feet high. They used an off-shore rig as a base for the workers there and those men used their equipment to build a reservoir to collect rainwater. They shipped in soil to cover a majority of the island, although the natural sea action had done a good job of creating beaches already. Then they flew over the island and sprayed various seeds and fruits, then let nature take its course. They also brought hogs, goats, cows, and a few other animals, although most died in the new environment. It looks like any other Pacific island now."

"But still—how could people survive?"

"A lot of the early ones didn't. But some did. All were given basic survival tools. You have to remember, Pat, the principle involved here was that this was to be a place for society's most violent misfits. No one really cared about their survival. Now there are villages on the island, governments, even law and order of sorts."

Pat was trying to imagine life under those circumstances and was having difficulty with the entire concept. "Who the hell came up with such a hare-brained scheme?"

"Time enough for that tomorrow," A.J. said. "I'm going to bed."

19.

Bonnie was taken to a cell she shared with no one. Only a few minutes passed when the matron returned with a woman dressed in a business suit. She was perhaps twenty years older than Bonnie. The matron said nothing but opened the cell and let the woman in. She sat on the edge of Bonnie's bed.

"Hello Bonnie," the woman said. She had a pleasant voice.

Bonnie just looked at the woman but didn't answer.

"My name is Susan. I'm a psychologist and my job is to help you with the transition. I'm sure you must have questions."

Bonnie still said nothing but she took a deep breath and her body shuddered.

"Why don't we start with the next few days," Susan said.

It was a statement, not a question. "There's a camera up there in the corner. You'll be monitored for the time that you remain here, for your own safety, of course. Meals will be brought in to you three times a day, and twice a day for an hour each time, you'll be taken to a day room. But don't be concerned with this routine. We expect to transfer you within just a day or two. When arrangements have been made, you'll be transported to California where you'll reside in a similar facility with similar rules. There, you'll be examined by a doctor and will be given information about Banishment Island. Your stay in California will be anywhere from just a few days to perhaps as long as three months. When the next ship leaves for the island you'll be on it.

"The island is only a prison in the sense that you can't leave it, and there is no communication with anyone off the island except the Capital Crimes Commission representative. I'm told the living conditions are reasonable and many prisoners would rather stay there than return to society."

Bonnie looked up from the floor and began quietly crying.

"Do you have any questions? No? Well, if you want to talk, just tell the matron and she'll fetch me." Susan was moving to the cell door but turned at the last minute as if she had forgotten something. "I almost forgot," she said. "Any member of your immediate family can voluntarily accompany you but they will have to stay for life, as well. Your husband, your daughter. Oh! I guess that doesn't apply in this case, does it?" She smiled wickedly as she left the cell.

Bonnie cried herself to sleep then dreamed of being abandoned on a deserted island. She awoke to the sound of a baby crying but when she sat bolt upright, there was no sound.

20.

Pat was driving. A.J. sat in the passenger seat with the seat slightly reclined and had his shoes off and his tie loosened.

"Last night you asked who originated this bright idea, or words to that effect," A.J. said. "I expect that was a rhetorical question but it is something you should know. His name was Tom Samsung. Father Thomas Samsung, ess, period, jay, period. That stands for Society of Jesus. He was a Jesuit priest. Dead now.

"I was there for a good deal of it and much of what I'll tell you probably isn't in the history books. Worse, I don't trust my memory to be entirely accurate. Worse still, I've never been much on religion so I don't want you to think that my impressions of Jesuits or priests or even Catholics, for that matter, is entirely accurate, either."

Pat reached over and turned the radio off.

"I met Father Tom at a party. It was a fund raiser for a judge that wanted to be re-elected and most of us were obligated to be there and I'd guess most of us would rather be somewhere else." A.J. stopped speaking and was clearly remembering events from a long time ago.

"Well, we met and we talked. Party talk. Nothing serious. I don't remember who introduced us." A.J. thought some more. "Anyhow, a day or two later, the judge who was eager to be re-elected called me and invited me to dinner at his home and wanted me there because this priest would be bouncing new ideas around and the judge wanted me to be a buffer. It was another obligation, but I went.

"Well, Father Tom had some ideas, all right. At the heart of it, he wanted to abolish capital punishment—the death penalty. This was at a time when all the major cities were in an uproar about crime, reform bills were on the tips of every politician's tongue, there had been riots outside of prisons where executions took place—it was a mess. To further complicate things, it was apparent to everyone that a rich criminal had a much better chance of acquittal than a poor one and I suppose that grated on Tom. The criminal proceedings were circus-like. Television broadcast the events live and the media fed a hungry viewer all the gossip they could dig up, with the attorneys providing gossip that was too difficult for the reporters to unearth on their own.

"The subject matter was right up my alley. And it turned out I liked Tom. I mean I really liked him. As a man and as an intellect.

"I never suspected one man would have the ability to force any change in our legal system so I never took our conversations seriously. I mean, the subject was serious, but what could one man do? It was like the days in college when we seriously discussed philosophical matters. It made for an interesting evening but we all knew there could be no positive change in the real world."

A.J. was silent again for several miles. He finally rubbed his eyes then continued.

"You're probably wondering what qualifications a priest would have to even seriously discuss law.

Crossed my mind, too, and that was the subject on many an evening.

"I'll tell you my impression but you have to understand, I don't know that this is factual. It's only my impression.

"Near as I could figure, a Jesuit's calling has little to do with saving souls or doing any of the other mundane things normal priests are apt to do. I think, or at least thought then, they had only one purpose and that was to pick a subject and learn as much about it as humanly possible. Then cogitate on what they've managed to learn. Twist it. Test it. Think on it some more. Then they get to expounding. It wasn't good enough to be the most enlightened man on earth if you didn't tell others what you had learned. At least, that was what I thought about Jesuits back then.

"Well, expound he did. And he was good at it. I eventually came to think that he was right about many of his ideas. At the core of his plan was a penal colony where violent criminals would be left to fend for themselves, permanently away from the rest of society. That plan would solve the death penalty issue, would remove repeat offenders from the streets—hell, there were a lot of good points.

"Some of the things we didn't completely agree on were the method by which the accused would be tried. We also had heated discussions regarding what constituted a capital crime. Tom's definition was simple: all crimes of violence. I was able to conceive of many acts of violence that were forgivable.

"I suppose it was inevitable that we compromised a great deal on those issues and sometimes I've wondered whether Tom wasn't leading me down his pre-ordained path.

"In any case, it came time to implement some of our ideas. By the way, I was not the only sounding board Tom used. He spoke long and hard with many other attorneys, professors, judges, senators—you name them and he talked to them. All he asked of me is my support as he went forward with the plan.

"Well, I'll be damned if he didn't get to the right people. Every once in a while I'd get a call from a senator or a professor or someone and they'd ask what I thought of such and such. I had told Tom I would support his ideas and I did. If one of the callers had changed the idea or didn't understand the concept, I was quick to put him back on track.

"Finally, the first bill was introduced as an anti-crime measure and it got a lot of press coverage and there was a lot of hoopla. But it passed. That first issue was a federal bill that offered any state that wished to become a party to it could do so voluntarily. Some did. A few years went by and other states were impressed with crime statistics that were being touted and they joined in the movement.

"Even though the whole thing made headlines in the beginning, it soon became a peculiarly quiet movement. I suppose the press didn't want to spend much space on good news. That doesn't sell papers or improve ratings.

The ironic thing is, Father Tom was killed by what they used to call a 'drive-by-shooting' only a few months after the bill was introduced and before it passed. He never saw the results of his efforts.

"You hungry?" A.J. said.

They ate in a small restaurant in Comins. They were perhaps forty minutes from home. The meal was good but they ate in silence. It had been a disturbing morning for them both.

When they were back on the road Pat was the first to speak.

"You said you had disagreed with the procedural elements of his plan. What were they?"

"Later. I need a nap."

That afternoon, A.J. sat at his computer which he had linked to a library network. He ran a printout of something, read it over, then went to bed.

21.

Over the next several weeks, A.J. continued to tell his story, usually one hour at a time, then insisting on a break.   Pat took notes and in some instances A.J. reminded him that he was working from memory and that Pat shouldn't take everything he said literally. After each of those occasions, A.J. would sit at his computer and linked to a library, produce some documentation that almost always confirmed the old man's story.

In July, A.J. abruptly told Pat the lessons are over.

"Spend the next ten days writing your brief," A.J. said.

"But remember, it's called a brief for a reason. Don't show off.   Don't get too wordy.   About ten pages would be right, but they'll need to be the best ten pages you've ever written.   Then go home for a week and try to patch things up with your girlfriend."

"Will you review it when I'm done?" Pat said.

"Nope. I've done more than I should've already."

22.

Bonnie was in a detention center in San Francisco. It was built especially for transients waiting for the trip to Banishment Island.

Each of the prisoners were held in one-person cells except for those who had families that were going to be traveling with them. Family cells were like miniature apartments but not well furnished. Neither inmates nor family members were allowed to visit other inmates or other families.

It was not completely uncomfortable but it was lonely.

The only persons Bonnie saw were psychologists and counselors. Some of the appointments were mandatory but she could see any of them at any time she wished.

The first few days were a blur. She couldn't remember any of the details of those days but she finally settled in and the routine had become familiar. She had been issued new clothing and had been to a survival class.

She was told that when she were transferred she would be given a month's rations and basic tools including cookware, a knife, a shovel, a saw, and other necessities. Each time the prison personnel offered instructions, she went to the classes but frequently feared for her future based on what she had learned.

They showed her a film of the island taken from the air and although she could see what appeared to be clusters of tents and huts, she kept imagining she would be forever exposed to the elements.

She understood now that this place she would be going housed the nation's most violent criminals and that there were no law enforcement officials to protect her. She imagined that her day of arrival would be akin to being thrown into a den of lions. Surely she would be raped repeatedly and be dead before the sun set on the first day.

During the third week in the transient prison, she was taken to see a matron who explained she was a para-legal— not an attorney—and she would provide Bonnie with the necessary forms and instructions to request an appeal to her conviction.

As soon as Bonnie heard the word appeal, all other instructions fell on deaf ears. She had been living in fear every moment since the police had come for her in her bedroom in Detroit. Finally, a chance to tell someone she was innocent, she thought.

Bonnie spent three days dreaming of an acquittal before she actually looked over the forms she had been given. She realized she did not understand how to fill them out or to whom to send them. She rang for a matron and asked to see the para-legal again.

She had to wait three more days for the para-legal to return and each day Bonnie thought that she wouldn't come back before the ship would leave.

A frightened and panicky Bonnie met the young woman with a rush of questions.

"How do I fill these out? Who do I send them to? How much time do I have? When…"

The young woman calmed Bonnie and answered her questions and even offered to assist her in getting things right. But there was no hurry. She could take care of it now or at any time in the future. Even on the island she would be able to communicate with the authorities.

They worked on the papers for several hours and when they had completed the application, the para-legal told Bonnie that within a short time someone would come to interview her and if that were successful, her case would be forwarded to a review board and then to an attorney who may or may not be willing to take her case. If it were turned down, she could re-apply on an annual basis.

"How long will it take? When will I know?" Bonnie said.

"Hope for longer. If you get turned down, the answer comes back rather quickly. The longer it takes, the better your chances are. Might be a year."

For the first time in a year, Bonnie felt the glimmer of hope. But it was clouded by despair. Even if things worked out, her life had been ruined. She gazed out the small bullet-proof window and saw a ship sliding up to a dock.

23.

The prisoners were each given a trunk that contained their belongings and their survival gear. Any personal effects could be taken, as well, but she had none. She wore ankle chains that connected to a waist chain. From the waist chain was another chain connecting to handcuffs.

For the first time Bonnie could see other prisoners but they were kept well apart. As far as she could tell, there was only one prisoner that had a family going with him. The woman carried a baby and she had no chains.

Inside the belly of the ship Bonnie was released from her chains and placed in a cell much like the one she had left. A male guard came by and told her she would not be allowed out of the cell for the remainder of the trip and that would be about 32 days, including stops that had been scheduled.

Bonnie paced the length of the cell. About eight feet.

She couldn't quite reach both walls with her arms outstretched. The door looked heavy and was made of steel with a smaller steel door in the center of it just below the small bullet-proof window which looked out into a hall. Directly across she could see a similar door and wondered who would be in that cell.

At the back of the cell was a stainless steel toilet with a sink built into the top where the tank had been on her toilet back home. Home, she thought. Would she ever see a normal toilet again?

Jack Radtke

On the right side of the cell and bolted to the wall was a narrow cot. It too, was made of steel with a two inch ridge around the edge and two inch holes in the base of the formed pan. Rolled up on the end of the bed was a thin foam rubber mattress and a folded wool blanket was on top of that. Opposite the bed was a stainless steel desk bolted to the wall but it was only about twelve inches wide. Below the desk a swing-out stool allowed someone to sit at the desk. She stepped to the sink/toilet and looked in the mirror bolted to the wall. Polished stainless steel. But it was the first time she had seen her reflection in some time. She had lost weight. Leroy would be pleased, she thought.

There was no glass so she cupped her hand, caught some tepid water and drank. She was resting her forehead against the cool of the mirror when a loud buzzer caused her to jump. Shortly afterward the small door in the center of the main door opened. The hinges were on the bottom and on the outside.

The guard placed a plastic tray with a meal on it.

There was a soft plastic spoon but no other utensils. A plastic cup had warm milk in it. She ate the peas first then the mashed potatoes. They were good. A piece of roast beef, too tough to cut with the soft plastic spoon, smelled good. She picked it up with her fingers and ate it all.

She put the tray back on the still opened miniature sideways door and stared through the small window. As she watched, a man across the narrow hall placed his empty tray on his small door.

"Hey!"

The man didn't even look her way.

The guard returned to pick up the empty tray.

"Put the cup on the tray," he said.

"Can't I keep it? There's no glass in here."

"The cup, lady. I don't have time to be visiting with you."

She replaced the cup and the guard snatched the tray away.

"If you behave, I'll leave the food pass open," he said.

"One bit of trouble and it gets closed for good.

Understand?"

"Yes sir."

When the guard left, she tentatively placed her hands through the opening. It felt a little like being free. She would give him no trouble.

24.

For the next several days the ship plowed its way through heavy seas. Bonnie was seasick and by the third day wished she were dead. Finally, on the fourth day she began to feel a little better and by that evening looked forward to a meal.

A week later she remembered the sickness and wished for it to return, if only to break the monotony. Every day she followed the same routine. The lights came on automatically. Shortly after, a buzzer sounded and then the guard brought breakfast. A few hours later lunch was served, then dinner. An interminable time later the final buzzer of the day sounded and then the lights went out.

She had tried several times to speak to the man in the cell across the hall but each time he turned away from his cell door. Perhaps he's deaf, she thought.

Bonnie respected authority even when the person holding the authority didn't treat her well. As a result, when the guard who brought the meals entered her cell one day and told her to move to the back of the cell and lean against the wall, she immediately did so. He had said it was a routine contraband search.

Before she realized what was happening, the guard slammed her face into the wall with his left hand gripping the hair on the back of her head, and with his right hand gripped the collar of her orange jump suit and pulled it down her back.

The top three buttons popped off and with the collar pulled nearly to her waist her arms were trapped. He spun her around and tore at the lower buttons and pushed her roughly to the floor. She banged her head on the edge of the steel bunk frame and was nearly unconscious. He's raping me, she thought.

The guard whispered coarsely through his gritted teeth.

"Keep your mouth shut and everything will be just fine."

Bonnie began to struggle and opened her mouth to scream but he hit her with the back of his hand before the first sound was uttered. She could taste blood swirling in her mouth then he was pushing at her, his whole body pumping. She could feel her flesh tearing as he entered her. She bit her lip to remain silent and wished Leroy were there.

When he was through with her he said, "Enjoy your dinner." Then he laughed as left the cell.

Bonnie remained on the floor for a long time and wondered what she might have done to deserve this. Finally, she went to the sink and washed as best she could. There was blood on her inner thigh and along her jaw and neck. Her lip was swollen and discolored and she had bitten herself hard enough to make it bleed, too.

She took the tray of food and sat at the small desk but didn't eat. She sat staring at the food and watched her tears drip onto the meat.

The guard returned to retrieve the tray but Bonnie still sat at the desk with it.

"Hey, bitch! Give up the tray. I ain't got all day."

When she heard his voice she whirled around and threw the tray toward the open food pass. It crashed against the door and food sprayed over the door and walls. The tray broke into several pieces.

"You'll be sorry you did that," the guard said, and then left.

Bonnie began picking up the pieces of the tray and began wiping the food off the door. Strangely, she felt as a child might who had just done something wrong. She began to cry again and still holding a shard of the tray sat on the edge of her bunk.

There was the noise of her cell door being unlocked and three guards entered the cell, one of which was the guard who had attacked her.

Without thinking, she lunged at him, screaming and trying desperately to stab him. The other two guards were able to grab her, take away the shard of plastic and move her toward the cot, all the while she was screaming.

"You bastard! You raped me! Bastard!"

The older of the two guards that were holding her grabbed her by the hair and tilted her face toward him. He turned to the rapist.

"Better get the chains. She's a wild one," he said.

As soon as the rapist had left he said to the other guard, "Charlie, she didn't get bloodied up like this by washing her face too hard. I'm taking her up to see the doc. When Mr. Hot Pants gets back tell him she calmed down and I took her to the warden and to meet me there. I'll call the warden before you get there and tell him what's going on."

He half dragged and half carried Bonnie down the long hall and then up a flight of stairs. Three doors down was a steel door with a pane of frosted glass mounted in it. The guard opened the door and pushed Bonnie in ahead of him.

"Hey, doc. Check this girl out. I think she's been raped. I got to use your phone."

When he hung up, he told the doctor that he would be in the warden's office and to call there as soon as he knew the girl's status.

The three guards stood in front of the warden's desk.

There wasn't room for three chairs.

"This is bullshit," the rapist said. "She threw her food at me. I just went in her cell and roughed her up a little, that's all."

The other men were silent.

"Really. I'm no rapist. You'll see. The doc won't find anything."

The rapist and the doctor were pretty good friends and when in port had been drinking buddies. He was counting on the doc to keep his mouth shut and then share a wink between them later.

The phone rang. "Yes?" the warden said. There was a long pause while he listened. The warden's face showed no emotion. Finally, he said "Thanks." He replaced the receiver in the cradle.

"Mr. Pillars, you are under arrest. You have the right to remain silent. Anything you say can and will be used against you…"

Mr. Pillars, the rapist, looked rapidly from one face to the next. The older guard was putting cuffs on him.

Bonnie spent the rest of the cruise in the ship's medical ward, sedated. She was unaware of the fate of Mr. Pillars.

25.

Pat submitted his brief and was invited to an interview.

The early part of the summer had passed quickly. In retrospect, he had gotten along just fine with his great grandfather. The old man might be a curmudgeon, Pat thought, but he's my curmudgeon.

The last two weeks seemed like an eternity. He had waited by the window every day for the mail to arrive but when news finally came, it was by telephone. His mother stood behind him, body tense, wondering if the news was good.

When he replaced the receiver, she said, "What? What? Tell me. What did they say?"

Pat grinned that quirky grin he sometimes used. "I don't know. I have to go to Harvard for an interview."

Strangely, it was his father who selected the clothes he would wear for the interview. He told his son that on the most important cases one should dress as if one were the president of the United States. This interview ranked right up there with his dad's important cases, Pat thought, so he went along with his dad's selection.

He stood before a glossy oak and leather trimmed table behind which sat three elderly gentlemen. They too, were dressed as if they were presidents.

"Your brief was exceptionally well written. Succinct," the first man said.

"However," the third man said, "it seems to center on Capital Crimes."

"Yes. Highly unusual," the first man said.

"Was not the assignment to demonstrate knowledge of the history of law?" The third man seemed to speak to no one in particular.

"Perhaps you could explain your approach?" This from the man in the middle who spoke without looking up from a stack of papers on the table.

"Yes sir," Pat said. "The history of law in this country seemed to require an exhaustive effort. One that would result in a book length document, possibly more, to do it justice."

"Justice. I like that. Good one." The third man was laughing a peculiar laugh. Sounded almost like snoring.

"Please go on," the middle man said.

"Yes sir. I apologize if I haven't met your expectations. I sometimes tend to focus on my goals more than most and it would seem I have erred."

"Nonsense. No error. We're here to determine if by this submission you're indicating that you intend to pursue a career in Capital Crimes, and if so, to offer you a doctoral scholarship. Providing, of course, you're up to the challenge and have the stamina, eh?" The speaker looked to the other two gentlemen who were both nodding. "Serious business, this Capital Crimes."

"Does this mean I've been accepted?" Pat said.

"Accepted? Well, of course. Accepted? Hah! Of course, of course. Yes, naturally. Didn't you receive the letter? Unanimous. Only three were this year—unanimous, that is."

Pat could barely believe his ears. Accepted.

It was a long but fruitful day. After an hour or more of discussion as to what led him in this direction and how he happened to be so knowledgeable on the subject, the three men took Pat on a tour of the campus and ended in a counselor's office. They discussed the curriculum and living arrangements, the need for a source of income in order that his energy wouldn't be deflected from his studies, and the benefits of a mentor. Perhaps he could find a capital crimes attorney to work with during periodic school breaks?

Pat knew just who to ask.

On the flight back to California, Pat thought about the scholarship. It was complete. Books, tuition, everything. What the scholarship didn't cover, the checks from the Commission would. He would be paid more than he thought possible to educate himself.

Then the somber thoughts entered his mind. What if he couldn't cut it? What if it turned out he didn't like the law? Perhaps hated it.

As soon as he had de-planed he headed for a telephone in the airport terminal.

"A.J.? They say I'll need a mentor."

26.

All of the prisoner's trunks had been off loaded and were piled on the dock. The prisoners, chained, were led into an auditorium and were briefed by two men who took turns speaking. Bonnie missed most of it because there was an echo in the room that made it difficult to hear. The only part she remembered was that they were permanently out of society and would be ignored forever more and that the only communication possible was through letters that could be sent to attorneys that were part of some Commission.

They were then led individually through a brick tunnel and were guarded by two guards with guns drawn after the chains were removed. At the end of the tunnel was a heavy steel door. There was a rubber walkway no more than eighteen inches wide and twenty feet long that went through an open gate in a tall fence. She was told to stay on the walkway. If she left the walkway or touched the fence, she would be electrocuted.

On the other side of the fence were a group of people dressed in rough looking brown and tan clothing and one man in an orange prison jump suit. They waited patiently for her to carefully walk through the fence opening. Before she crossed through, she turned for one last look at the guards, but the steel door had already been closed.

She looked fearfully at the people waiting for her.

They were smiling and reached out with their arms. When she walked through the gate, several people grabbed her and pulled her within the group and many of them began to hug her.

The man with the jump suit stepped forward and introduced himself.

"I am David," he said. "And you are?"

"Bonnie. Bonnie White."

"Very well, Bonnie White. Welcome to Regenesis. Mary and Sue will take you to your quarters, if you'll be kind enough to walk with them." He wrote her name on a piece of paper, using a stub of a pencil. "We'll bring your trunk to you in a little while."

"Mary and Sue chattered away at her while they walked but Bonnie was overwhelmed with the new sights, sounds and smells. It was hot and very humid. There was a stone sidewalk and on both sides of the walkway were huge piles of square stones. In the distance she could hear someone hammering against the stone with other stones.

Suddenly the piles of stone dwindled to nothing and a jungle seemed to cover everything. Even the walkway was narrower here. Bonnie could hear strange birds but couldn't see them.

The path began to widen and eventually the jungle opened to a clearing in which was located a picturesque village. Some of the buildings were made of straw and sticks with palm leaves for a roof and a few were made from the stones Bonnie had seen earlier. There was one large building in the center made of stones. It, too, had a thatched roof.

There were a few older people who strained to see the new woman in the orange jumpsuit and a group of children, many of them naked, ran along behind them. They seemed happy.

The three women worked their way through a maze of smaller huts and finally entered one of them. They shooed the children away and Mary faced the center of the small one room hut and spread her arms and hugged Bonnie again.

"All the fears you've had, the scary dreams, the loneliness, it's all over now. You're among friends," Mary said.

"Yes. It's true," Sue said. "We're a sad lot."

"Murderers, thugs, rapists. But we get along. You'll find Regenesis a pleasant place to live."

"Get that orange thing off. Here's a nice dress for you to wear till your trunk gets here," Mary said. "Sue, drop a hammock for Bonnie. I'm sure she wants to rest a little." Turning to Bonnie, she said, "You'll want to be rested before the festival tonight."

Both Mary and Sue gleefully clapped their hands and left Bonnie alone in the hut. Moments later she could hear the two women playing with the children who had waited outside.

Bonnie was awakened by Sue. "You should get up soon.

We'll want to pretty up a little before the festival begins."

Bonnie had fear in her eyes and it took a moment to realize where she was. She swung her legs from the hammock and let the hammock swing to and fro. Finally, she noticed her trunk on the floor. It surprised her. She had thought it would be stolen. There was nothing in it of importance but it represented her total worth. Without it she would be nothing.

27.

The three women entered the large stone building in the center of the village. There were perhaps three hundred people present. Mixed in the crowd Bonnie only saw one orange jumpsuit and that was worn by David. She occasionally recognized a fellow prisoner by the pale complexion. Of course, there were many black people in the building and she had no idea whether they were prisoners or not. Silly, she thought. We're all prisoners.

There was music being played but the tune was unrecognizable. She liked the primitive beat. Many of the people had drinks in cups that looked like they had been made from coconuts.

The laughter and buzz of conversation stilled and Bonnie looked around to see what was happening. David was standing on something in the middle of the room that made him taller than the rest.

"Can I have your attention," He shouted.

The drummer beat his drums in a crescendo of noise.

"Welcome to Regenesis," David said. "For our new friends, I'd like to point out that there are no guards or wardens looking over this festival. You are all free people, equal in all respects with everyone else here tonight." The crowd roared their approval.

"This festival is in your honor, new friends. It is an opportunity to get to know some of your neighbors and an opportunity for the rest of us to get some news from home. I sincerely hope you don't feel badgered by all the requests you'll probably receive tonight." There was a general excitement building in the audience.

"There is, however, a few things I feel compelled to explain in order that we all get off to a good start.

"We are all here—all of us—because we committed a crime against society—a violent crime. Now, most of us are innocent, naturally." There was general laughter from the crowd. "But seriously, consider that if all of us are capable of violent crimes, how safe can we be among ourselves? For this reason we have developed our own laws with our own punishments. We trust we will all get along. If, however, we do not," David paused for emphasis, "You will find our justice is swift and sometimes brutal.

"During the weeks that follow, our new friends will be instructed in the laws of our land. In the meantime, follow the laws as they were written in your hometown. They will suffice nicely for the time being. Should we discover cases of insanity among you, and we all are familiar with that defense," David paused while a wave of chuckles swept the audience, "You will be moved to a different community and will be humanely cared for.

"Now... enough serious business. Let the festival begin."

The band began playing a merry tune and many of the people who had been squatting on the dirt floor stood and began to dance. Others began rushing toward new faces in the crowd, excitement evident on their own faces.

A terribly fat woman, several years older than Bonnie, rushed up, sweating profusely, her face beaming. "Can you sing?" the woman said. "I hope you know the words to some new songs. I have the choir, you see…"

The fat woman was interrupted by an older gentleman wearing a white beard. "This is August," he said. "You must have left in late June or early July. How are the Dodgers doing?"

Before the gentleman even finished his questions three more people were vying for Bonnie's attention. She felt flustered, out of control. She wanted to escape, but Susan came to her rescue.

"Hold on," Susan said. "She can talk to all of us.

Please. Let's sit here in a circle and only one question at a time. Henry, would you be a dear and get three of us something to drink?"

The older gentleman with the white beard scurried away and the rest of the people began to sit at Bonnie's feet.

"This is Bonnie White," Mary said.

"Hi, Bonnie White," they said in unison.

"Have a seat, Bonnie," Mary said.

"Before our enthusiasm overwhelms her," she said to the small group, "Perhaps Bonnie would be good enough to tell us something about herself. Then we can ask questions about what's going on in the real world."

As Bonnie spoke, several more men arrived and quietly sat at the fringes of the group.

"…and this whole thing has been a nightmare for me.

I heard everyone laugh when David said some of us are innocent, but I really am." Bonnie finished this with a plaintive note in her voice.

The group was silent and just stared at Bonnie, some in open disbelief and a few with sympathy in their eyes.

"We'll help you file a notice for appeal," one of them said. "But I wouldn't feel right giving you any hope that it'll do any good. I've been here six years and I've filed the paperwork for myself and I've written many letters to the Commission and they never even acknowledged them."

After he saw the look on Bonnie's face, he amended his opinion. "Of course, I'm not really innocent and it does sound like you are, so we'll try. I'll come by to see you tomorrow."

Henry had returned with drinks and another man brought fruit and passed it around.

Bonnie tasted her drink and decided it was good. It had the burn of alcohol but it tasted like a sweet, fruity wine. She said she liked it and several people told her how they made it. It was a mixture of fruits that had fermented then been strained. It had no name. They just called it a drink.

They were beginning to laugh again and the questions came singly, each person raising their hand to be noticed. Mary selected the questioners and kept things orderly.

After their initial enthusiasm for information had been satisfied, Bonnie was even able to ask a question occasionally and the group responded enthusiastically. If nothing else Bonnie was beginning to feel relaxed and accepted.

There were many more men than women and there were lots of children, but none seemed to be over twelve years old so she asked about the strange mix.

Since this society was not comprised of normal birth rates and new members were continually being imported, it was only natural that there were an abundance of men. That generated one of the first rules of Regenesis. Single women lived in a separate area from the others, as did the single men and the married families. Children were raised by the community and were free to sleep wherever they felt comfortable, frequently with the single women. When a child was thirteen they left the community and lived separately learning skills the community would need for its survival, such as farming, sewing, hunting, fishing, building skills, and tool making. When they reached twenty one, they returned to the community.

They each had work assignments according to the skills they possessed and the skills required by the community. All the profits of their efforts were shared equally. The following day, new huts would be built for the newcomers and all who had the skills would assist in that effort.

The explanations of daily life on the island were interrupted by David's presence. The group clearly deferred to him. When they were silent, David spoke. "Part of the festival is to get to know each other but a bigger part is just to have a good time," he said. "Looks like this group is entirely too serious." He turned to Bonnie. "Would you care to dance?"

She hadn't danced in so long she wasn't sure she remembered how. Then she thought of Leroy. "I shouldn't," she said.

"Nonsense. It's part of the acceptance ritual" David had a warm smile and Bonnie felt she couldn't refuse, so she went with him to the dance area.

"Don't worry," he said as he swept her about the dirt floor, "I think you'll like it here."

"I miss my husband," she said.

David didn't speak to her again but as they moved about the floor, he frequently spoke with others who were dancing, and each time, made a point to introduce Bonnie. She noticed many of the men danced together.

"Are they gay?" she said.

"No. Not at all. They've discovered dancing is fun and there's not enough women to go around. It's just harmless fun."

"But there are women. More than I would have expected, if I had thought about it. Have they all been convicted?"

"Of course not." He acted surprised at her question.

"Most were born here. Some came with their husbands and a few, like yourself, were convicted of some crime." He smiled again.

"There's not many people here, either," Bonnie said. "Is this all of us?"

"Almost. There's the youth camp and the asylum. All together, we're just over four hundred."

"I would have thought there'd be lots more," Bonnie said.

"Well, the biggest single problem we have is disease.

"The Commission is supposed to screen new persons coming in for communicable diseases, but sometimes…" David seemed less cheerful for a moment. "Our last outbreak was nearly three years ago. Nearly six hundred died. We had a doctor among us, but no medicine." As the music stopped, he bowed to her and began walking her back to her group. "But don't worry. We eat well and we take care of each other. I hope you'll come by to visit me from time to time."

Suddenly, David was in the middle of the room again, standing with his arms upraised. "Let us give thanks for this wonderful evening. Tomorrow we'll need a few volunteers to clean up. Sleep well!"

In two's and three's, everyone strolled into the night.

"Perhaps I could help clean up tomorrow," Bonnie said.

"Oh, no. That'll be done by others. We each do what we can do best and there are a few that are handicapped who look forward to helping to their own ability. It would not do for an able-bodied person to take their jobs away," Mary said.

"But I should do something to help."

"What did you do before? Did you work?"

"I was a mother." Bonnie's eyes glistened with the memory.

"Well, then. You can work at the nursery. They always need help and you'll be appreciated, too."

Bonnie had trouble falling asleep that night. She worried about taking care of babies. She might not be able to hold a child without crying for the loss of her own.

28.

Pat was immersed in his studies. He had never considered how much library time would be required. At this rate, he thought, I'll need glasses before I finish up here.

Once again, he discovered a new word which he would add to his vocabulary. Many of the terms used in legalese were Latin. Some were French.

"Damn!" he whispered, "Why can't they just use English."

The person seated next to him said, "Tradition, I suppose."

Pat had been so engrossed in his work he didn't realize anyone had been there. Surprised, he look up. "Sorry. Didn't mean to disturb you."

"No problem," the young girl said. She looked around.

"I think we're the last ones here, anyhow. I'm Brittany." She held out her hand. "My friends call me Britt and my best friends call me Bratt."

Her hand felt cool but her grip was firm. "Hi Britt. I'm Pat, to friends, best friends and even to enemies. Are you first year law, too?"

"Yeah. What a deal, huh?"

"I guess," Pat said. "How do you like it, so far?"

"I think I'm at the beginning of a love-hate relationship."

"Me too." Pat looked at his watch. "I think I've had it." He began to gather his things. "Care to join me for a coffee?"

"Sure. I have to walk by the coffee shop, anyhow."

Britt was a tall girl, eye to eye with Pat. She stood erect and walked with a long gait, matching Pat with ease. Her hair was long, dark and straight. She had a direct personality. No coy glances. When she spoke with him, she made positive eye contact. Her eyes were dark.

"I haven't seen you around," she said. "Not even in the library. What classes are you taking?"

"Only three, this term, but they're a bitch. Oops. Sorry."

"That's okay. Mine are, too. A bitch, that is." She had a nice smile.

"The one that's giving me the most trouble," Pat said, "has been Psychosis and the Serial Killer. Not bad enough studying law, now I have to be a psychologist, as well.

"We have to look up serial killer cases and then discuss the psychological aspects of the accused and determine, no, not determine, but justify... yeah, justify the defense used in the case.

"What really gets me is there's no right answers. We talk forever and, bottom line, it's whatever anyone thinks is right is right."

"You sound," she said, "like a Capital Crimes candidate."

"Yeah. How'd you know?"

"Been considering it myself."

They turned into the crowded coffee shop. Sitting across from Britt, Pat could see now that her eyes were not just dark, they were luminous.

They talked for some time about the classes they were taking and how many more stretched ahead of them. That was the main reason Britt was hesitant to committing to the Capital Crimes curriculum. She worried about spending all those years in education when she could be out earning a living. She was curious about how Pat could afford this kind of education.

"I'm on a scholarship." he said.

"No kidding. Smart, huh?"

"Just average, I'd guess," Pat said. "Actually, I don't even know why I got a scholarship. I was counting my blessings just being accepted. It was a real surprise when they offered me a free ride, not to mention income."

"Income? What's the deal?"

He told her about his brief and the ensuing interview which had culminated in the scholarship offer.

"A poser," she said.

"What? What the hell's a poser?" Pat said.

She had an infectious smile. "A poser is a puzzlement. Something nearly impossible to understand. As in 'this poses a problem'. Ergo a 'poser'.

"I'm going to check this out," she said. "If I could get a deal half as sweet as this, I'd opt for J.D.C.C. in a heartbeat. My dad's working two jobs and my mom works, too. It's all they can do to get me through this year. I've even been wondering if there'll be a 'next year'. Are your parents broke?"

"Nope. Well off, I guess. My dad's an attorney and he does okay. My mom's never worked, except around the house."

"Maybe that's it." she said. "Your old man's got some pull."

"I don't think so. I mean, he even tried to talk me out of this." Pat thought for some time. "Like you said. A real poser."

Britt drained her coffee and began gathering her things. "You're nice," she said. "Here."

She passed him a paper with her phone number on it. "I live off campus. Call, if you want. Maybe we can study together." Then she was gone.

Pat stayed for a few minutes thinking about Britt. She seemed nice, too. He didn't think he wanted any relationships, but Britt just seemed like somebody he could be friends with. Maybe he would call.

29.

Over the next several weeks, Bonnie had moved into her very own hut and had begun to feel a part of the community. She had her job at the nursery and enjoyed the children even though it was a continuous reminder of her own lost child.

At the end of her normal workday, she spent the evenings with some of the other women. They had invited her for coffee, but it turned out their version of coffee was some ground roots boiled in water. It was a little bitter but it was good. They spent their time chatting, mostly about life back home at the insistence of the native women, but worked while they talked. They made hammocks and sometimes pottery. They sewed and they sometimes made more food than they could possibly eat in one or two meals. On those occasions, they looked for somebody who could use the extra food and were always able to find someone thankful for the gift. Some evenings they just played with the children who always seemed to be present.

It was on one of those evenings when they were sewing, using homemade needles and coarse thread stripped from a jungle vine, that they heard a commotion nearby. They followed the noise and saw a man struggling between two other men. They were dragging him away, and many of the women from this small part of the community were following them.

"What's going on?" Bonnie said.

"I don't know," Susan said, sounding puzzled.

The parade continued through the women's area, then through the married's area, and finally stopped at a stone building near the community building.

Although the crowd was doing its best to be reasonably orderly, there was some noise and commotion, simply due to the large number of people who had followed the threesome.

David stepped from the door of the stone building. He looked somber. "What is it?" he said.

"Caught this man stealing," one of the two men said who had been holding the squirming man in the middle.

David looked at the man in the center for a long minute. "Take him to the community building."

When they arrived, David sat in a chair made from branches of a tree and woven palm leaves. "Tell me what you witnessed."

The man on the left told of finding the thief in the hut of a family and he had several of that family's possessions under his arm and preparing to leave.

David addressed the accused. "You have a reason for this?"

The accused told David that he was only recovering items which he had loaned to the family. Things that were rightfully his.

David asked who lived in this dwelling. The man on the right said, "Betty and Harry, of Delaware."

David dispatched four of the men who were watching events unfold to find Betty and Harry.

While they waited, the entire crowd was silent. The accused stood looking at his feet and shuddered occasionally.

After waiting for perhaps fifteen minutes, Harry was brought into the building and stood before David. David said, "Harry of Delaware, do you know the accused?"

"No sir. I've seen him before, but do not know him."

"Have you borrowed goods from him that remain in your possession?"

"No sir. I am not inclined to borrow. And certainly not from someone I don't know."

When David next spoke, it was to the two men who had brought the thief before him. "What, precisely, did you witness the accused taking from Harry of Delaware's residence?"

"A staff, David. Hand carved. And a hammock."

"Very well," David said. "Let the crabs eat his hands. Perhaps useful tools can be made from his bones." David stood.

Bonnie watched the crowd nodding agreement with the decision and moved with them through one of the many doors in the large building. They walked to an area of the beach that she had never seen before. There, the two men held the prisoner by both arms with his hands stretched over a stone retrieved from the piles she had seen when she first came to Regenesis.

With a single blow from a machete, David sliced through the man's left wrist. A second blow severed his right hand at the wrist. The hands lay in the sand, fingers twitching.

The man screamed.

"Bind him well," David said as he turned to leave.

Several people from the crowd that had followed stepped forward. They had already gathered wide

123

leaves from the plants that grew alongside the path that led to this place. They quickly placed the leaves over the bloody stumps and packed mud made with sea water and sand over the leaves. They added several more layers of leaves and mud and bound the crude bandages with thin vines. They left the now unconscious man on the beach. Another man picked up the twitching hands from the sand and tied more vines securely around them leaving a length of vine trailing behind. The hands he threw into the sea and anchored the vine to rocks on the shore. In three days, the hands would only be skeletal remains.

When the machete fell, Bonnie moved to the side of the crowd and vomited on the sand. Both Susan and Mary helped her to walk back to their hut.

That night, Bonnie couldn't stop thinking about the severe punishment meted out. She questioned Susan about the fairness of the punishment, how the thief would be able to live without hands, why David was the one to make the decision. There were many things she didn't understand.

Susan and Mary only said that David was fair and that his decision was sound. The man would be cared for by the community but would be encouraged to learn a new trade in order to be a contributing member of the community. There would be no ill feelings toward him. He had already paid for his crime, and experience showed that it was unlikely that he would steal again.

Bonnie never saw the man again and was afraid to ask what had happened to him. Had she asked she would have discovered he had survived, and was working with the youth of the community as a teacher, at the recommendation of Harry and Betty of Delaware.

30.

Bonnie had written her third request for an appeal. The first time, she had eagerly accepted help from the white haired gentleman she had met at the party, but it turned out that there were no complicated forms to fill out. Simply state the reason you believed an appeal was in order in your own words and then walk back to the stone piles where she had arrived and place the letter in a mail box. The box was vacuum activated and the letter was sucked away to be read by the Commission.

The third letter was longer than the others and in it she implored the reader to at least acknowledge his receipt of her correspondence. She had also outlined the reasons that she should be considered for an appeal. Even as she wrote the words, she realized her reasoning sounded shallow and without merit.

Bonnie supposed she had already resigned herself to a life on Regenesis. It wasn't so bad, she thought. She had made some friends and life was peaceful. She had yet to explore the island, so perhaps she wasn't quite as comfortable as she tried to believe. That's it, she thought. Tomorrow she would begin walking the island. Maybe Susan or Mary would come with her.

It had been a pleasant day at the nursery. There were twelve children who actually needed full time care. The others were old enough to play by themselves and there were two older women who watched over those children. As Bonnie watched the sun lowering over the trees that surrounded the nursery clearing she began to anticipate their adventure. Susan and Mary had both agreed to join her.

Finally, the three women who watched the children during the evening appeared on the path. Bonnie half walked and half ran in her excitement to begin exploring.

Bonnie, Sue and Mary walked through the married area first and Bonnie was surprised at how many of the men and women she recognized, though she couldn't remember their names. She waved a greeting and returned their smiles as they walked.

Bonnie had relaxed a little but felt the tension returning when they approached the next clearing. The men's quarters were ahead. She needn't have worried. Although this area was much larger than both her home area and the married area combined, there seemed to be few men walking about. Susan explained that many of the men had physically difficult tasks and were probably already sleeping. Unlike the single women or the families, in this area was a central eating area. They had cooks that prepared two meals each day and all the men ate together. Bonnie wondered aloud why they rated special treatment. Mary told her that the men needed good nutrition if they were to continue with their labors and that the treatment wasn't special, it was necessary.

The path made a wide arc to the north after leaving the men's living area and after more than a quarter mile ended in the school area. There was one building with no walls and several benches for the children inside under the thatched roof. Bonnie saw no books, no blackboard, and no teacher's desk. There was, however, a large clay bowl with several pointed sticks in it. "What are those for?" Bonnie said.

"The teachers use those to write in the sand," Mary said. "We have no blackboards or chalk."

"What about books?" Bonnie said.

"A few. But they're closely guarded. The head teacher brings them to school every morning and takes them home every evening. None are really school books, though. All we have is what people brought with them and most of those aren't fit for kids to read."

If I ever get out of here, Bonnie thought, I'm going to send books here for the children. Suddenly, she missed reading more than anything, even though she had only read magazines when she was free and then, mostly looked at the pictures of movie stars.

Bonnie walked through the classroom, imagining what it must be like to be a student here. She paused near one end of the building, where the remains of today's math lesson was still scribbled in the sand.

"C'mon," Mary said. "We'd better start back. It'll be dark soon."

"Do we have to be back by dark?" Bonnie said.

"No. But we won't be able to see much either."

As they walked back, they took a new path that bypassed the living areas and came out on a beach. They walked the shore back to their huts.

"Tomorrow's Sunday," Bonnie said. "Can we go out again tomorrow?" All day?"

"Sure. Right after services. Where would you like to go? Anyplace special?"

"I don't know," Bonnie said. "What else is there?"

"Oh, we could go to the quarry, or the hospital... I know. Let's go to the reservoir. We'll take a picnic lunch and on the way we'll show you the asylum and the hospital. We can see the quarry any time." Mary jumped up and down and clapped her hands.

31.

"There's the hospital," Susan said. The three paused and looked at a building very similar to the schoolhouse. Bonnie could make out perhaps six people lying in hammocks and two others walking about.

"We're not allowed to go any closer, just in case there's anything contagious down there," Susan said. "We don't have any medicine, but we send the patients the best of our food—vegetables and fruit and whatever meat we can afford. The nurses grind up some roots for fever and infections but they don't always work." Susan was silent for some time. "Most people who come down sick, die. It's a wonderment that the nurses don't die, too. Must be because they do the Lord's work."

As they continued climbing the path Mary broke the silence to show Bonnie the cemetery. It was unbelievably small.

"Is this all there is?" Bonnie said. "I thought David said more than six hundred people died just a few years ago."

"They did. We don't actually bury anybody here. We place their body in the sea. The crabs take the flesh and we retrieve the bones. Many of them are useful for tools. The cemetery only has death boards in it. You know, the names and the year that each person died. Maybe someday we'll go down and look at them."

The path continued to climb a circuitous route up the hill on the center of the island. They came to a fork and Bonnie asked where the other path led. "We can go there, "Susan said. "I mean, it's allowed. But nobody wants to. "C'mon."

"That's the asylum path," Mary said.

A short distance later they were able to hear screaming and moaning carried by the ocean breeze. It sounded animal like. Not human.

"Did you hear that?" Bonnie said, but neither of them answered.

They came to a spot where the path led along the side of the hill with the view to their left unobstructed. They stopped and Susan pointed to a clearing some distance away. "The asylum," she said.

They could hear the screams clearly from here. There were scores of cages about eight feet square, each with a lone occupant. Most of the men paced inside their small prisons. Some climbed on the wooden stakes that made the walls and the roofs. Others were lying motionless. All were naked. There were very few cages that were empty. Walking among the cages were several guards, all carrying either machetes or clubs.

"This is terrible," Bonnie said.

"Not terrible. Humane," Susan said.

"But there's no treatment."

"We have no one that is trained to care for them. At least not their minds. But they're treated kindly. Given food and water."

"But if no one is trained… Who decides that they belong here?" Bonnie said.

"David. These are the ones that are violent. But they can't help it. They need to kill or to hurt. It's for our own safety. C'mon. We shouldn't have brought you here."

Bonnie was as terrified now as she had been the first day. She continue to follow her two friends but could think of little else after seeing the asylum. Small muscle spasms caused her to shudder occasionally as she remembered the animal-like screams. Strangely, neither Susan or Mary seemed affected by the caged men.

The path had leveled and they seemed to be on a plateau.

Occasionally they could glimpse the sea through small thinnings in the brush. Ahead, they could hear laughter. The sounds of families at play.

Susan and Mary burst into the clearing surrounding the reservoir and raced to the water's edge. There were several families nearby and they had mats with picnic supplies spread on them. Bonnie walked slowly to the mat her friends had spread and slowly sat, hugging her knees and staring out over the man-made lake.

There were several posts placed in the ground with palm leaves attached to make umbrellas to shade them from the sun. Bonnie's friends unpacked their lunch and several of the children came to their mat bringing with them coconuts that they had been using as balls. Soon Mary and Susan were running and playing as if this were just another splendid day in paradise. Bonnie got up and began slowly circling the lake.

Half paradise, Bonnie thought, and half hell. And I'm stuck here. Forever. She began to cry.

32.

Britt was explaining to Pat that she had been turned down for her scholarship, but that she was free to try again twice each year. The scholarship was not awarded based on academic merit or on need, although both would be considered. The primary thing, she said, was that you needed to show commitment. She had to admit, as she had done with the interviewing board, that she was not ready to commit. At least, not yet. It was a decision that should not be taken lightly and she had the integrity to give careful consideration to her feelings and to be honest with the board. At least they had invited her to try again.

Pat put his arm around her shoulder. It was not a romantic hug, but a re-assuring hug given to a friend, but still with a lot of affection.

"How did you know," Britt said, "And how did you convince them that you were ready?"

"Actually, I didn't know. At least until right now. I mean, it wasn't until you started telling me about this that I realized I am committed to finishing this thing. Beats me how the board knew how I felt before I even knew it."

"Well," Britt said, "I've got all summer to think about it."

"Does that mean you'll be back?"

"Yeah. My dad looked into some deal with the union. They've got some program that will finance members' children at no interest. If I sign up with the union after I pass the bar and give their members free counsel, they'll waive one year's loan for each year of service I give them. If not, I have to pay them back. But at least it's interest free."

"Well, that's a break," Pat said.

"Yeah. Well, it sounds good but it doesn't feel right. And I'm sure not looking forward to creating a debt that competes with the national debt."

"But it means you can come back next year."

She looked at him strangely, then winked at him. "Sure. Sounds like you're being a little selfish." She smiled. "Don't worry. I'll be here."

"C'mon. Let's study. What have you got left?"

"Only one verbal and I'm ready for it. You?"

"I've got this brief," Pat said, "And one verbal that needs some work. Could you proof the brief for me while I do a little reading?"

"Sure," she said. "Help me with this cork."

They sipped wine and studied for the next three hours.

When Britt looked up from the brief she had been proof reading, she saw that Pat had fallen asleep. She kissed his nose and left a note for him reminding him that tomorrow night she would like his help packing.

Two days later, Pat had submitted his brief and they had both given their verbals. They shared a cab to the airport even though Pat's flight left six hours after Britt's. He would still be waiting in the airport when she arrived back in Pittsburgh where she would spend the summer clerking at a small law office.

He planned on returning home for two weeks, then driving back to Michigan where he would work with the local prosecuting attorney, gratis, and live with A.J.

He planned on leaving his car there when he returned to school next year and would continue to live and work with A.J. as long as he was allowed to do so.

Britt's plane was being boarded. He walked with her to the boarding gate. They stood facing each other and held hands. Neither knew what to say.

Finally, Pat broke the silence. "I think you're my best friend." It surprised him to realize it.

"I'm glad."

"Well," Pat said, "Stay out of trouble." He squeezed both her hands and gave her a small hug, cheek to cheek.

"Yeah. Right. You watch out for those bears." She squeezed his hands back and then she was gone.

As he watched her plane taxi away from the gate, he thought, I'm really going to miss her.

Jack Radtke

BOOK TWO

Jack Radtke

1.

It had been seven years. Bonnie could no longer remember the date, not even the month, of her arrival at Regenesis. Tonight they were welcoming a new group. The ship had come in two days ago and they had begun to wonder if the passengers would ever disembark. All day yesterday they had waited at the gate but no one came through. This morning over a hundred began making the scary trip down that threatening tunnel. Three were families. In just an hour David would make his little welcoming speech. By midnight, he would probably select a third of this group to be housed in the asylum. It still saddened her to think of the conditions there.

Living with David and bearing his son had changed her outlook on many of the things on Regenesis and given her a new understanding of what a caring man David truly was. But the asylum still gnawed at her. On many other issues she had some influence with David but on the asylum, he was adamant.

She had been through many of these welcoming parties in the last years but tonight she had butterflies in her stomach. She had received a letter from the Commission—her third—and she had not yet mentioned it to David.

"Bonnie. Aren't you ready yet? We still have to take Lee to the nursery." David stood behind her and encircled her with his arms.

Lee, she thought. Leroy. When he was born and she said his name will be Leroy, David had objected. That was no name for a civilized man, he had said.

Sounds like a red-neck name. But she had insisted. In memory of her husband. David had understood, but he never called him Leroy, only Lee.

She had to admit, David was a good man, perhaps better than Leroy had been, but she had been in love with Leroy. She could never have explained the difference in feeling she felt for Leroy and for David. She loved David, but she had been 'in love' with Leroy.

David leaned forward and kissed her forehead.

He was a tall man, at least by Bonnie's standards. His hair was nearly completely grey now and lines had formed on his forehead, and at the corners of his eyes. The scar at the corner of his mouth, so prominent when they had first met, now looked like just one of several wrinkles. He was not yet sixty but the texture of his skin had suffered from years in the tropical sun.

Back home, Bonnie thought, he would be too old for me, but here, on Regenesis, what did age matter. She watched him walk outdoors.

How would she ever tell David. The Commission had seen fit to forward her case to an attorney for possible appeal. The man would be examining her case even now. At least she thought of him as a man. It might even be a woman attorney. He/she would arrive in the next week to interview her. And that scared her.

David had understood her need to continue trying for an appeal. He even believed in her innocence. But would he understand that if she were to be freed... Even the thought terrified her.

"Bonnie! It's late. Let's go."

She scurried from the hut they shared, saw David holding Lee and smiled in spite of the pressures she felt. She thanked him for being patient with her and kissed Lee on the forehead. "C'mon, little man," she said to Lee. "It's time to visit with some of your friends."

Lee struggled to get back on the ground and walk himself but Bonnie said, "Daddy's late and we have to hurry. Mom'll carry you."

As they hurried down the path to the nursery, Bonnie brought up the subject of the asylum, again.

"How can you be so arbitrary? In one evening, I don't see how you can just watch these people then decide who's crazy and who's not."

"Crazy is not the issue," David said. "I watch their behavior, their eyes, how they watch the others. I try to mingle with them and have some conversation. And 'crazy' does not fully explain what I see in some of them. It's more like the look of a predator. And you'll have to admit, there have been damn few acts of violence from those who remain in the community with us."

"Sure," she said. "How do you know half or more of those you lock up wouldn't fit in just as well?"

They had reached the nursery and she kissed Lee good-bye. He smeared away her kiss with the back of his hand and was already running to meet his friends.

"We've been over this before. I'd rather err on the safe side." His tone suggested the discussion was over. As he walked away, she had difficulty keeping up with him.

As they entered the community building, Bonnie skipped to catch up and said, "I want to meet the men you send away."

David glared at her but when he faced the people his face broke into a warm smile and he made his way to the center of the room with his left arm about Bonnie's waist and his right arm waving greetings to the many friends and neighbors gathered there. As he stepped onto the platform he whispered to her, "Stay by my side then."

David gave his speech welcoming the newest members of the community. It hadn't changed much since the first time Bonnie had heard it, except now, he introduced her as his wife and paused while the crowd cheered for her.

She didn't know many of the people, not as one knows a good friend, but she was always friendly toward everyone and it seemed they all liked her. In fact, the general consensus was that she was very good for David and if she was good for their leader they would have liked her regardless of any personality flaws she might have had.

David finished his speech and they began to mill through the crowd. Many had already started dancing and little pockets were formed around the newcomers as there had been on each of these welcoming parties.

David made his way to each of the newcomers, welcomed them individually and introduced his wife. With most, he shook their hands, spoke a few words, and moved on. Every once in a while he allowed himself a little more time and spoke at length with a few of them.

Bonnie was alert to any nuances that might indicate she had been speaking to a 'predator' but had begun to feel at ease. There were some she didn't like, but most just seemed to be ordinary people who were a little frightened. She did what she could to make them feel at ease in the few moments she had with each of them.

At one point, they found themselves out of earshot and she said, "So far, so good, huh?"

"Three so far," David said.

She quickly turned back to look at the men they had already spoken to but couldn't determine which three.

"C'mon, I'll buy you a drink." He grabbed her elbow and steered her toward the table with drinks and snacks laid out. "The ones that I hug or place my left hand on their shoulder will be gone by midnight."

"Oh, my God," she said. "I wondered what was wrong with me. Each of the men you made a fuss over I didn't like at all and wondered why you thought they were so special."

"They're only special because they strike me as being so dangerous that I want them gone tonight. There will be others that will take me several weeks to ferret out."

"What if you make a mistake?"

"I'm as careful as I can be, balancing my heartfelt opinion with the knowledge that if I miss one, some friend of ours will end up murdered, raped, beaten. I take this selection very seriously." He was smiling broadly at the man serving drinks.

"Evening, David. Fine turn-out tonight," the man said.

"Yes, it is. Two drinks, please. And one for yourself."

David handed Bonnie her drink and they walked toward a small group which seemed to be badgering a pale young man with questions.

"I think I see what you're looking for," Bonnie said, "but I don't think I could do it. I'd be too concerned with making a mistake."

"Remember this, then," David said. "There was no one on that boat except the truly innocent who haven't already committed a violent crime. The asylum is no worse, and I dare say, possibly a far sight better, than their fate would have been had they been locked up on the mainland. I believe you were raped by a guard, were you not?"

He said this with no malice intended. In fact, his voice was gentle as he reminded her that conditions could be much worse.

Bonnie put her hand softly on his forearm. "I'll pray that you make good choices, then. And I'll leave you to your work."

2.

One of the rules of Regenesis was to accept or not, the person you see standing before you for what he is today and for what he might become, for on Regenesis, there is no past, only a future.

It was a noble thought and the underlying meaning was that it was forbidden to ask about one's past. Should someone choose to tell you of a past life, that was acceptable. But it was not acceptable to be so bold as to ask. The punishment for such boldness was thirty days excommunication from the community. It was correctly taken to mean criminal past. It was not only okay, it was considered polite to ask where folks were from, if they had family, what careers they left behind.

As a result, Bonnie had no idea what crime David had committed. She had hoped he would confide in her but she refused to ask and he had never volunteered. She had, however, told him about her early life, and she sometimes wondered if his belief in her innocence was merely based on his love for her or if her story had been that convincing.

This afternoon, only two days after the welcoming party, she chose to tell him of the pending visit by a Commission attorney.

"David, you know some of us are innocent."

"I've told you, I do the absolute best that I can. If you know of a better way, please tell me." He was instantly angry.

"I was talking about me," she said quietly.

"Oh. I'm sorry. This is always a difficult time for me." He looked tired but walked toward her and embraced her. "Forgive me?"

"Sure." Lee had joined them and was hugging Bonnie's legs. "Go outside and play, Lee. Mommy and Daddy want to talk for a few minutes."

David watched his son go and slowly released his embrace and moved his hands down Bonnie's arms until he had clasped her hands. "What's up?"

She squeezed both his hands and looked into his eyes.

He doesn't deserve this, she thought. "You know I've written several times to the Commission asking for an appeal."

David leaned away from her at the waist and cocked his head and lifted one eyebrow.

"I got an answer," she said.

Both David's eyebrows shot up and a slow smile creased his face. "Well? Do I have to drag it out of you? What did they say?"

She turned her eyes away. "There's an attorney coming to meet with me. He probably came on the ship. I'm supposed to meet him at the gate."

David was laughing. "No way. Watch for a small jet. He'll come by plane." He stopped laughing but the smile remained. "How long have you known? Why didn't you tell me?"

"I couldn't. What if, you know. What if I get an appeal. I'd have to leave. Leave you."

"Time enough to worry about that. If it took seven years for them to just answer your letters, imagine how long the appeal will take." He dried the tears rolling down her cheeks using his thumbs then gave her a great bear hug. He laughed again and swung her about the small room.

"A celebration. We have to celebrate. The whole community…"

Bonnie was sobbing now. He pulled her to the floor and hugged her tenderly, trying to soothe her fears away.

They talked well into the night interrupted only by Lee asking permission to stay at Susan's for the night. David had been supportive and talked her through all the emotional issues using reason and logic and sometimes dark humor. He told her he would be dead of old age before the legal system finished with her. She had punched him in the stomach with her elbow.

They finally got to specific near-term problems, like how would she know when the attorney had arrived, and did she have to leave the island right away, would Lee go with her, who would handle Lee while she was with the attorney. She found her mind had questions to ask faster than she could speak.

David didn't know the answers to any of her questions.

He told her that in the entire time he had been on Regenesis, not one person had ever been interviewed by an attorney. Several had been through the appeal process and were kept informed by letter, but no one had ever had a personal visit.

He still wanted to have a celebration but she insisted on keeping it a secret, if possible.

3.

David had arranged for one of the newly arrived mothers to take Bonnie's place at the nursery. For two days David and Bonnie had patiently sat at the arrival gate waiting for some news. On the third morning, two remarkable events occurred. The ship left and with it, Bonnie was sure, the attorney who had failed to keep the appointment, and a red light began flashing on the mailbox. Neither David or Bonnie was sure when the flashing began. It might have been signaling them for hours or it might have just started.

David rose, looked over his shoulder at Bonnie, then walked to the mailbox and opened it. Inside was a blue envelope addressed to 'Bonnie White'. Below her name were a series of numbers that were meaningless to them. Inside was a note that simply read 2:00 PM.

They both looked toward the sun. Perhaps three more hours. They spent the time in nearly total silence, leaning against each other, shoulder to shoulder.

Finally, a flashing beacon over the tunnel door. The door opened and two uniformed, armed men stood in the opening. "Bonnie White?" one man shouted.

Bonnie stood but did not move any closer.

"The fence gate will open in a moment. When it does, come forward, alone. Do not touch either the gate or the fence. Walk only on the rubber walkway. Do you understand?"

She nodded. A moment later, the gate began to move.

She turned to David, fear and apprehension in her eyes. He put an arm around her shoulder and squeezed. "Good luck," he said. "I love you."

Both guards pointed their weapons in David's direction.

He stepped back a couple of paces. The guards relaxed.

When Bonnie reached the guards, one of them passed his weapon to the second guard then placed chains around her wrists, waist and ankles. She watched David as the man completed this task. The door closed and she was led down the nearly forgotten tunnel. At the end, a female guard searched her then joined the other two guards and led her to a building on the docks.

Bonnie experienced a strange feeling and wondered if this was the feeling of freedom. She was still on the island but was now on the other side of the fence, with all the ramifications that that passage held for her.

The guards opened the door to the building and gently pushed Bonnie inside. There were two men seated behind a table, bare except for a single leather briefcase. One of them sat in a wheelchair and he was very old. For a moment, Bonnie thought the younger of them must be a nurse.

"Are you Bonnie White?" the older man said.

She nodded affirmatively.

"My name is Ripplestone. A.J. Ripplestone. This is my, um, my associate, Pat Ripplestone. We would like to discuss your case and possibly offer representation. Can we do that? Discuss your case, that is?"

Bonnie's cheek twitched and she could feel her stomach churning. "Yes sir."

"Good. Good." A.J. stared at her for some time. "Have a seat. We may be together for some time. Might as well be comfortable." His smile seemed to relax her a little.

He turned to Pat. "See if you can get a guard to do something about those chains. And get us some breakfa... perhaps lunch would be better." He turned back to Bonnie. "Hungry?" Without waiting for an answer he said to Pat, "Make it three lunches."

Bonnie hadn't heard a plane arrive but thought they must have arrived by plane. It was probably three o'clock by now and the old man wanted breakfast. Probably jet lag.

A.J. didn't speak, but watched Bonnie with something approaching a smile. A guard came in and wordlessly began removing Bonnie's restraints. The guard left.

"Well," A.J. said, "when Pat gets back we can get under way. In the meantime, let me say we have reviewed the legal aspects of your case and find nothing untoward. Everything is in order. We also checked the transcripts, both written and tapes, and we viewed the videos of your trial. Actually, we were at your trial, although it was for an entirely different reason than what you might imagine."

"Lunch will be here shortly," Pat said as he re-entered the room. "They're also seeing to a more comfortable room for us to meet in. Real furniture."

"Good," A.J. said. "I've already explained to Bonnie that there is no legal reason to examine her case.   No mistakes made upon which to hang our proverbial hats, so to speak."

"Then why did you come," Bonnie said.

A.J. smiled.   "While watching your trial, Pat thought you were innocent.   'Course he hadn't even started law school yet." A.J. reached over and jostled Pat's shoulder.   "In fact, he still hasn't finished law school. But he will." A.J. smiled. "Pat is this close to a doctorate."   He held up two fingers spaced about a quarter inch apart. "When I die, or possibly am forced into retirement, Pat will take over this work. Our job is to look into cases like your own, for instance, to determine if an injustice has been done, and if so, to correct it."

Lunch arrived. For the first time in seven years Bonnie ate from a real plate with real silverware. And there was salt. And pepper. And real milk out of a real glass.

Pat and A.J. spent the entire time that they ate in idle talk, asking Bonnie about life on the island in order to help her relax and feel comfortable talking with them. When they finished, A.J. suggested it was too fine an afternoon to spend indoors. Bonnie thought that meant she had to return to her hut, but A.J. had a walk in mind. The guards allowed it but followed them at a discrete distance.

A.J. removed a miniature microphone from his pocket and attached it to his lapel. He handed one to Pat and one to Bonnie. "Just so we won't have to take notes," he said. "The recorder is in my briefcase here on my lap." He turned to Pat and waved him forward.

Pat pushed A.J. down the path by the sea and Bonnie walked next to them. "Tell me," Pat said, "about your family — parents, brothers, sisters."

"Okay. I had only one sister. No brothers. Her name was Marie."

"Excuse me," A.J. said. "I notice you said 'had'. Has your sister passed away?"

"Oh, no. I don't think so. We just get used to talking about everyone in the past as if they were dead. It's part of life here." They walked on in silence for several moments.

"My sister was my best friend in the world. She was a few years older than me, but we were close. She taught me everything. Just everything." Bonnie looked out over the breaking waves. "My dad was okay. I guess he drank too much but he was an okay guy. He is dead, by the way. He died while I was in jail in Detroit, waiting for a trial. My sister wrote me.

"Anyhow, where was I? Oh, yeah. Mom was nice but I think she was afraid of Dad. I didn't think so then, but looking back…"

The sun was setting and as they made their third trip by the few buildings where some of the civilians worked, one of the guards suggested they enter one of the buildings. It was a day room, with game boards, a small library and an entertainment center along one wall. Coffee with cups were on a tray on a table in front of a couch covered in plastic.

A.J. struggled to get out of his wheelchair and sat in a chair. Pat and Bonnie sat at opposite ends of the couch.

Bonnie had been talking for nearly two hours and the two men learned quite a lot about her early years and had a sense of what her life must have been like. She had not mentioned Leroy.

"I feel as though I've known you for years," A.J. said. "And we appreciate all you've told us. Tell us about your husband, Leroy. How did you meet?"

Bonnie continued her long story with a far away look in her eyes. She had gotten to the part where they were living in the truck parked on a side street in Detroit and Leroy was getting desperate to find work when A.J. suggested they get some rest and meet again in the morning for breakfast.

Bonnie spent a restless night in a strange room.

Sleeping in a real bed again was not the pleasure she had thought it would be. It was too flat, too hard, and too warm. She missed David, she missed Lee, and she missed her own hammock.

The next day, the attorneys allowed her to continue her story, mostly without interruption, even though she glossed over the deaths of her husband and her daughter.

After lunch, the mood changed subtly and both Pat and A.J. began asking questions. Their interest centered not on the crime scene, as she had thought it might, but on the names and addresses of acquaintances in Detroit, Leroy's employer, where the guns came from. It seemed to her that she had answered each question as fully as she could, but they insisted on re-asking the same things over and over. They were not hostile, as the police had been, and in fact, were gentle. Gentle but focused. Sometimes the questions changed so that she was halfway into the answer before she realized they had already asked the same thing several times before. Sometimes they would be talking about simple things, like her daughter when suddenly one of them would say something like, "What was the caliber of the gun Leroy gave you?"

She began to think they didn't believe her and were trying to trip her up and she began to cry.

Pat slid toward her on the couch and put an arm on her shoulder. "It's not that we don't believe you," he said. "Our questions and the manner in which we ask them will allow voice analysis later and that will help us greatly. If we didn't believe you, we would have never made the trip here to see you."

"Perhaps some rest is in order," A.J. said. "We can take a little break. I could use a nap anyhow. We'll meet for dinner, then afterward, I'd like to try hypnosis. What do you say? A short nap sound good?"

"Sure," Bonnie said. She dried her eyes on the handkerchief Pat offered.

Bonnie saw David sitting cross-legged in the saw grass that grew near the entry gate and she ran through the gate and threw herself at him.

He held her close for a long while. "Was it bad?" he said.

"No. Not really. They were nice men. There were two of them. It was just hard remembering…"

David helped her to her feet and he continued to hold her as if she were too weak to stand alone.

"They hypnotized me, too," she said.

"What are they going to do?" he said.

"I don't know. They said they'd be in touch. And they gave me this." She held up a card. "They said they would make arrangements that I could write directly to them at this address without going through the Commission and without censorship. That's a good thing, isn't it?"

4.

The small jet was climbing rapidly into the blue sky.

In just a few hours they would be in Hawaii where they would change to a commercial airliner for the flight back to the mainland and then back to Michigan.

A.J. took advantage of the air time to write the first letter to Bonnie. He thanked her for her full cooperation and assured her that they were convinced of her innocence but that it would be a long and difficult struggle to gather the necessary information to warrant a re-trial. He would keep her informed of their progress and in future letters would describe in some detail the steps that were necessary for her freedom. He folded the letter, placed it in an envelope and sealed it.

"Pat, would you post this when we land in Hawaii?"

"Sure."

"You seem a little depressed," A.J. said. "What's on your mind?"

"Oh, nothing and everything, I guess. She's as innocent as they come if you discount her naiveté in entering that marriage and allowing herself to be brought into her position. On the other hand, we don't have a single solid thing to go on. I'd like it a whole lot better if we could find just one little flaw in the judicial process. Frankly, I don't know what to do."

"There's plenty to do, Pat. Even if you were finished with school and I were as energetic as I were twenty years ago, it could still takes years to track down everything we need to discover about Bonnie White.

"Do you think your friend Britt might be of some assistance?"

"She's certainly capable enough," Pat said, "but she'll probably be going back to work for the summer and she still has some time to go before she graduates."

"Yeah, but I've been thinking about that. In just a few months, you'll be finished and there's no good reason for you to continue working with our local prosecutor. Why not attack this Bonnie White thing full time and we'll see if we can set up Britt with our prosecutor. Think she'd go for that?"

"She can't hold a job and work on the White case, too."

"Why not? You did."

Pat thought that over for a minute or two. "It wouldn't hurt to ask, I guess. She'll have to pass the Michigan bar."

"I'm sure she'll have no trouble with that. Why don't you call her when we get back." A.J. studied Pat and thought, he's got the jitters. It would be good if his first case turns out to be successful. "Let's get started. Take the court transcripts and listen to them carefully. Make a note of everything you would have liked the defense attorney to have brought up, no matter how trivial it may seem. I'll do the same thing with the tapes of the interview with Bonnie, looking for anything she had to say that wasn't completely covered in the trial. By the time we get home we'll have a decent list of things to begin our investigation with."

"I've already done that," Pat said. "How about I pick apart the tape of the hypnosis session? That seems like more fertile ground."

"Okay."

Pat and A.J. needn't have worried about Britt. When they arrived at A.J.'s cabin, Britt was waiting for them in A.J.'s study.

"Great news," she said. "I've decided to take the Michigan bar. I mean, how tough can it be? Then I can practice right here and work with you guys in my spare time."

Pat and A.J. silently looked at each other and they both smiled.

"What brought that on," Pat said.

"Oh, I've been thinking," Britt said, "You're almost finished with school and it's going to be lonely without you there pestering me all the time to help you pass. So, even though I still have a ways to go, the least I can do is spend my summers and my breaks with you guys. You're not going to get rid of me just by getting a doctorate. And how would you ever get anything done without my help?

"Besides, I was notified yesterday that the Commission finally believes that I'm serious. I've been awarded a full scholarship, including income, just like the deal that you got. I needed a mentor, anyhow, so why not the two favorite men in my life?"

"Pat, get a bottle of champagne and three glasses," A.J. said. He turned to Britt. "And just in the nick of time." He opened his cracked leather briefcase and brought out five notebooks filled with nearly illegible scribbling. "Make three copies, one for each of us. Tonight we'll tell you about our trip and tomorrow we'll start assigning tasks from our notes. How long before you have to return to school?"

"Three days," she said, accepting the tall glass from Pat.

5.

Britt's assignment was to find the missing people in Bonnie's life. Her parents, her sister, any high school friends, Leroy's mother, neighbors in Detroit, and as many acquaintances as were possible to trace. From these, discover other friends, relatives, and acquaintances. Let the web grow till she knew more about Bonnie's family and friends than Bonnie did. In the process, she would be looking for character witnesses from those who knew Bonnie before their move to Detroit. From those she had met in Detroit, she would try to learn any new facts that had not been presented at the trial.

Britt began with Bonnie's parents but ran into dead ends. Her first successful contact was with Mrs. White, Leroy's mother. Britt tread lightly, not knowing if Mrs. White might hold Bonnie responsible for Leroy's death. But her worries were unfounded.

Mrs. White had thought that the kids' marriage was a 'storybook romance' and she was sure that Bonnie was innocent. The lady was a hopeless romantic. She could shed no light on anything leading up to the murders but she had saved several letters that Bonnie had mailed her years ago including pictures of Bonnie and Leroy. She even had one of her grand-daughter, and agreed to make copies of the letters and send both the letters and the photographs to Britt. There were hints of marital troubles in the letters, she had said, but nothing serious. Certainly nothing that would lead to murder.

Britt was able to obtain from Mrs. White the last address for Bonnie's sister, and she had been helpful remembering some of Leroy's friends, although Leroy and Bonnie together, hadn't made any friends that she had known about.

Britt agreed to accept letters from Mrs. White that she would forward to Bonnie. Leroy's mother agreed to testify to Bonnie's good character, if necessary.

The entire telephone conversation had been taped and Britt carefully transcribed the information, labeled it and filed it in a banker's box she kept in her bedroom. She mailed a copy to A.J.

The following Tuesday, Britt had only one morning class and most of her school work had been caught up so she called Marie, Bonnie's sister.

Marie was amazed to hear that Bonnie was alive. She had lost track of her sister so thoroughly that she had presumed she had died. The news brought many tears and blubbering and Britt was unable to gain much in the way of useful information, except she did discover Bonnie's mother's phone number and address, and told Marie she would call her again. Once again, she agreed to accept letters to be forwarded to Bonnie.

This time, Britt made some personal observation notes at the bottom of the sheet on which she transcribed the taped conversation. She couldn't help but wonder why Marie didn't know her sister's whereabouts and thought her strong reaction had been unusual.

That same afternoon Britt called Bonnie's mother. That conversation went on for hours. The woman was more than willing to discuss every aspect of Bonnie's family life and disclosed that although she had no proof, she was convinced that Bonnie had been sexually molested by her father who was now dead.

Britt wanted to learn more about the father/daughter relationship but there were no hard facts, just innuendo. Bonnie's mother remembered the father staring lewdly at both his daughters when they were not completely dressed. She remembered him 'accidentally' entering the bathroom when one of the girls was in the tub. The father was a heavy drinker and was a stern man, especially toward Bonnie.

The woman rambled on, providing Britt with considerable insight regarding Bonnie's home life. It was after Bonnie 'ran off' with Leroy that her father had died.

He had come home drunk, in itself not unusual, had gotten into an argument with Marie, the older daughter, who ran out of the house, then began beating his wife. During the confrontation, he suddenly went pale, clutched at his left shoulder and collapsed on the bedroom floor. The wife calmly sat on the edge of the bed and watched her husband die. She waited to make sure he was dead, felt for a pulse and found none, said a short prayer of thanks, then called for an ambulance.

As soon as the insurance money had been paid, she moved to Florida offering to take Marie with her, but Marie elected to stay.

On this transcription, Britt wrote: 'Avoid testimony. If jury thinks Bonnie learned from mother, she's as good as guilty.'

The final term of the school year had passed quickly and Britt was armed with a list of thirty seven people who had known, or knew of, Bonnie White.

She would soon be meeting with Pat and A.J. to determine a plan and she intended to suggest that many on her list required a personal visit. She also wished to obtain affidavits from several of them.

During this last term, Pat had no scheduled classes.

His only task, although a formidable one, was to complete his doctoral thesis. In the last three years, he had published two books dealing with schizoid personalities and capital crimes. Although he had been criticized for moving the philosophies of the Capital Crimes Commission backward, both books were now used as texts in graduate level work.

His doctoral work was an extension of his previous writings and he had moved to Detroit to complete this work, primarily to be close enough to the crime scene to follow up on Bonnie White, but he also spent many hours in the University of Detroit Law School Library as well as in the Wayne State University Library, both institutions becoming well known for their forward thinking in the two fields in which he was gathering data.

Whenever he found his scholastic research had temporarily overwhelmed him he would pursue Bonnie's case.

He had visited the White's old neighborhood on many occasions and had even canvassed on a door-to-door basis, all the current residents. On some of these occasions he actually felt as if his life were being threatened, simply by being there. He was developing a sympathy for Bonnie's lifestyle.

He had run into so many uncooperative people, several times he had thought of simply giving up. It was at one of these low points that he met Clem's father. Pat had been standing in front of the old tire business, now closed, hands stuffed in pockets and wondering if Leroy had actually worked there. He thought at his next opportunity he might check the business records to see if he could track down the owner, when an elderly man began to speak to him. It was Clem's father.

They walked to the diner where Leroy had used his last coins to tip the waitress before walking down Seven Mile Road to get that job.

Over coffee, the old man told Pat that he definitely remembered Leroy. "Damnable shame, his wife going bonkers like that and killing Leroy and the kid."

It was a rewarding conversation and the old man's reluctance to testify didn't dampen Pat's spirits in the slightest. This was the first positive piece of information they had yet gathered, the owner's father and an employee willing to admit that Leroy had been an employee, refuting the word of the prosecution.

"If old Bobby hadn't sold Leroy that piss-ant gun, Leroy might be alive today," the old man said.

Pat was so excited he could barely contain it. "Who's Bobby?" he said.

"Oh, just one of those punks used to come to work just to get enough money to make a score. Drugs." He looked both ways to see if anyone might be listening. "He's dead, too. O.D.'d."

"Damn. I'd sure love to have talked to that man. We could surely use proof that the gun was owned by a junkie."

"Well, you got my word on it," the old man said. "Saw him hand it over my own damn self."

Pat spent the next hour convincing the old timer that his testimony would be invaluable and that he wouldn't get himself or his son in any trouble by doing so. He also paid him a hundred dollars for his trouble and told him he would want to talk with him again.

Pat hurried back to his car and found it up on blocks, tires gone. Worse, his cell phone had been taken.

He hailed a cab and went directly to his apartment, called A.J. first, then a towing service, then the police.

A.J. would leave first thing in the morning and the two of them planned on cornering Clem's father to get a deposition just in case he was run over by a car or shot dead before they could get to trial. If possible, A.J. was even more excited than Pat.

When they talked to their only valuable witness, he had lost interest in testifying. A.J. assured him that he would personally see the prosecutor and the judge and felt confident he could get them to agree to waive any charges against either their witness or his son, Clem, in exchange for his testimony. Finally the old man agreed. They looked up the nearest law office, explained their circumstances and hurried over to have the deposition taken, witnessed and notarized before the old man changed his mind again.

That night Pat and A.J. composed a letter to Bonnie telling her they had some positive news. Not enough to file a motion for a trial, but certainly enough to give them, and her, they hoped, the encouragement to continue fighting.

Pat agreed his next task was to track down Bobby's friends and family. Having experienced a broad daylight car trashing he decided he would be maneuvering in neighborhoods that were more than he could handle. He imposed on A.J. to use his influence in police circles and was able to retain a streetwise detective to be his partner in the search.

6.

Detective David (Knuckles) Bradshaw was about three inches shy of six feet but he weighed two hundred and fifty pounds or more. He had tattoos on both arms and on his hairy chest, which was visible beneath the leather vest that he wore opened. His hair and beard were long, dirty and uncombed. He had a gold tooth and an earring. His vest had a motor cycle club insignia on the back which he referred to as his 'colors'.

He looked Pat over. "We've got work to do, laddie.

First, we're going shopping. Then we're going to get you good and dirty. Don't have enough time to grow some hair so we'll have to shave your head. Maybe a nice tattoo, right up there on top."

Pat could not imagine what he was getting into.

Knuckles doubled over into an exaggerated boxer's stance and threw several jabs that fell short toward Pat. "Just kidding. About the tattoo, I mean. It'll wash off."

"No way," Pat said. "I'm not shaving my head."

"Touchy, touchy. Okay. No haircut. I'll have to give this some thought." Knuckles was enjoying Pat's discomfort. "I got it. Do you know the Bible?"

"Not very well. I mean not enough to quote it or anything." Pat wondered what Knuckles was up to.

"C'mon kid. I think I can help you out."

Knuckles drove a motorcycle with a side car and together they careened around corners, Pat white-knuckled in the passenger compartment. When Pat realized they had stopped, he opened his eyes. They were parked on a sidewalk in front of a church.

Knuckles turned off the rumbling machine, pulled his helmet from his head, swept his hands over his beard and hair and started walking toward the front doors. He poked his head inside and shouted. "Padre!" There was no answer.

They walked around the side of the church and found a small building with a brass plate next to the door that read rectory. Knuckles leaned on the buzzer.

A tottering elderly woman swept the lace curtain aside and peered out. She opened the door tentatively. "Yes? Can I help you?"

"Tell the padre Knuckles is here."

The old woman gently closed the door and they could see her shadowed form through the curtain making her way down a hall.

A young but silver haired priest opened the door, smiled and stood back for them to enter. "Knuckles. You okay?"

"Yeah. We need a little favor. Y'got a minute?"

Twenty minutes later they were riding again, the wind parting Knuckle's beard down the center. They parked behind a red brick building and went in through the back door.

"Police properties building," Knuckles said.

He didn't introduce Pat to the young officer, but told the officer he needed some colors, same as his, but with 'Padre' embroidered on the back. To Pat he said, "Probably take a little while. We'll go get you a helmet made while we're waiting. This next stop, they don't know I'm a cop, so don't blow my cover. Just keep your mouth shut. Be cool."

Pat was beginning to feel a little more relaxed in the side car. They stopped at a used car lot and walked into the mechanic's area. Knuckles slapped one of the workers on the back.

"Yo! Knuckles. Where you been, man? Haven't seen you in months."

"Yeah. Been riding." He swept his palm over a newly painted street rod. "Nice ride."

"It's fresh and it's clean. You buying?" the man said.

"I'm buying. But not anything on four wheels." Knuckles motioned toward Pat, who was still standing by the doors. "Padre, here, needs a new brain bucket. Seems I got carried away and lost his in the Detroit River last night. Can you help me out?"

The man squinted toward Pat. "Yeah, sure. Have anything special in mind?"

When they left, Pat was wearing a newly made custom helmet that looked very much like the caps parish priests sometimes wore. It was called a biretta. The model worn by priests was made of a stiff black material and was round at the head band but square at the top with fins defining the line from the center to the four corners. The model Pat now wore was made of metal, was painted bright red and featured a long streamer that was attached at the center and hung down his back. The metal portion had been riveted over a standard plain-Jane fiberglass helmet.

In the alley behind the properties building, Knuckles took the clothing he had gotten from the priest and threw it on the ground, kicked it and stepped on it several times then gave it a cursory dusting before handing it to Pat. "Put on the vest and roman collar. C'mon."

Once inside, Knuckles retrieved a leather jacket, well worn and grimy with the word 'Padre' on the back. Even the new stitching looked worn and dirty. "Nice job," Knuckles said. "Put it on," he said to Pat. He looked Pat over, then turned to the officer behind the counter. "Got any ratty jeans? And we'll need some boots, too."

"All I got is cowboy boots," the young officer said, leaning over the counter to look at Pat's feet. "Might be the right size."

When they finished, Pat looked the part except he was too clean. Knuckles told him to go home, change his oil and not to wash afterwards, make sure there was grease under his nails. "It'll be dark where we're going. Maybe no one will notice."

"Um, no car. It was stripped and now it's in a garage being repaired." He gave Knuckles a sheepish look.

"Well, my bike needs to be tuned. You can help me and that'll get you looking better. Maybe that's not a bad idea. You can fill me in on what we're looking for while we work."

The first thing Knuckles did at his run down house was to grab six beers. He opened two, and poured half of one of them over the black vest that Pat was wearing. "You need the smell," Knuckles said.

He also loaned Pat a cheap watch mounted on a leather watch band three inches wide, a wide black leather belt, and a chain which attached to the belt and to his wallet at the other end.

Pat told him about Bobby while they worked and drank beer. The man had sold a gun that had been used in a crime to his client. Bobby was dead, but they needed to find someone who knew him and could verify that the gun had been sold and that it had been used in a crime. Not just any crime, but a specific armed robbery. Nearly eight years ago.

"Man, you got to be fooling with me." Knuckles couldn't believe they were chasing some small time punk over an eight year old crime. A punk that was dead on top of it.

"Well, there's one more thing we'll be looking for," Pat said. "About that same time frame, a young black male who broke into a house and took a gun from a woman, shot at her and ran off."

"Man, you got to be crazy. There's no way we're going to find anything."

"Maybe not," Pat said, "but we're going to try."

7.

Knuckles and Pat watched two movies on TV and drank beer. Pat was impressed with Knuckle's capacity.

Shortly after midnight, Knuckles woke Pat. "Time to ride," Knuckles said.

Pat wandered down the hall looking for the bathroom. As he was closing the door he heard Knuckles shout, "Don't comb your hair. And don't wash." And in a lower voice, "Damn rookies."

Knuckles handed Pat a worn bible. "Try not to lose it. It was my mom's. When we get there, hold that bible in your left hand up close to your chest. Yeah. That's it. I'll do all the talking. You just tag along and try to look stupid. It'll help if you grin a lot.

"If anyone insists on talking to you, just start quoting from the bible. It don't make any difference if you get it right or not. It'd be better if you screw it up. And every time you do that, I want you to giggle a little, but in a low voice. If they think you're a little crazy, we just might get through this."

Knuckles kicked his machine into life and they were off.

At their first stop the curb was crowded with other bikes. There were two scantily clad women leaning against the doorway and they eyed Pat with interest.

"Keep grinning." Knuckles said under his breath.

"Are they hookers?"

"No. Biker mamas."

Knuckles pushed one of the women aside and strode into the doorway. The other woman put her arm around Pat's waist. "Aren't you the fancy one," she said.

"The Lord will smite thee and turn thee to stone, sinner. Hee, hee. Get thee behind me."

The woman seemed to shrink away from Pat and let her arm drop from his waist. The other woman yelled, "Fuck off, asshole."

Pat turned toward her, gave her his version of a priestly blessing, and disappeared into the building, close on Knuckle's heels.

There was a bouncer in the dark hallway. He turned a flashlight with a red lens toward Knuckles. "Yo, Knuckles. Who's your friend?"

"My cousin, Padre. Padre! Meet Robot." To Robot he said, "Just ignore him. He'll be okay."

Robot swung the light toward Pat.

Pat kept grinning and peered over Knuckle's shoulder into the interior of the bar. He felt as though there were centipedes crawling down his spine but he said, "...and the Lord turned water into wine, lest the fish and bread be eaten dry."

Robot shook his head. "Go on in," he said. "I see what you mean."

They walked through a dimly lit area with cigarette butts on the floor. When they got to the bar, Knuckles kicked a stool aside and leaned forward. "Two that float."

The bartender brought two glasses of beer and two shots of whiskey. He took the shot glasses and gently dropped them into the beer. "Four bucks," he said.

Jack Radtke

Knuckles laid a twenty on the bar, picked up his drink and drank the whole thing down. When he looked at Pat, his eyes were watering. "Down it, Padre," he whispered. "Everyone's watching you."

Pat managed to down the drink but didn't trust himself to talk.

A man dressed much the same as the others, but clean and well muscled, said into Pat's ear, "You think you can just walk into my place like you own it?"

"Amen, brother. And the brethren shall flock to see Him. Wherever two or more of you are gathered in His…" "He's with me," Knuckles said.

"Hey, Knuckles. How you been?" The man slapped Pat on the shoulder. "I didn't mean anything. Just don't trust strange faces hanging around. You know how it is."

"Yeah, sure," Knuckles said. "We're looking for Basil. You seen him around?"

"Not lately. Don't come in here much, anymore. You might try over at the Hog Farm. Hey. Tell you what. Have one on the house before you go." The man lifted his muscled arm and Pat saw the tattoo on his forearm twitch when he snapped his fingers at the bartender.

As Knuckles and Pat roared down the street, Pat leaned over the edge of the sidecar and vomited.

"Jesus! A couple of beers and you're getting sick on me," Knuckles said.

"Not the beer," Pat said, rubbing his arm across his mouth. "Fear."

174

First Knuckles laughed. Then he said, "You want to quit?"

"Nope."

Knuckles told him that most of the men in the bar they had just left were decent law abiding citizens. They had normal jobs, families, went to church. They just liked being bikers. The crazies were in the minority.

Three stops later, they found and spoke with Basil and he enthusiastically agreed to help with their search. Basil was a staunch admirer of Sherlock Holmes, the movie version. As a result, he assumed the name Basil, after Basil Rathbone, the actor who had played the role for so many years. Basil, the biker, fancied himself a private detective, although he wasn't licensed.

When Knuckles dropped Pat at Pat's apartment, it was nearly four in the morning. Knuckles suggested they allow a week or two for Basil to come up with something.

"Do you really think he can?" Pat said.

"Nope. But then, if anyone can, it would probably be Basil. Don't shave. I'll call you in a week or so."

8.

A.J., Britt and Pat were discussing their progress. Pat had told them of his adventures in the world of the bikers and Britt was amused by the story. A.J. brought them back to the present by pointing out that Pat's foray may have been filled with excitement but it had been fruitless.

The mood turned somber but A.J. admitted that the search for Bobby's past friends and any confirming knowledge of the handgun being used in an armed robbery was probably futile. He encouraged Pat to continue the search but to be careful.

Britt had obtained a substantial number of sworn statements that could be used and had gotten agreements from many in Bonnie's past to testify if needed. The picture these old friends and acquaintances painted was certainly not of a killer, at least not one that deserved the attention of the Capital Crimes Commission.

A.J. had searched out old police reports and had interviewed the attorneys that had been involved in Bonnie's case. He had not been able to discover anything other than apathy among those responsible for ensuring the legal system worked.

They concluded that everything Britt and A.J. had come up with or were likely to discover would not be enough to warrant a new trial. The key to Bonnie's conviction had been the fact that the gun she had used had been traced to a previous violent crime. In order to undo that conviction, they would have to show that the gun may have been involved but she wasn't. That left only two choices. An alibi for her for the date of that crime, or proof of someone else's involvement.

A.J. made plans to return to visit with Bonnie. He would take with him a police psychologist who specialized in hypnosis. Between them they would examine the date in question in such detail that they would know "how many times Bonnie peed that day and whether she washed her hands afterward."

A.J. instructed Pat to continue his search but to let Knuckles concentrate on the biker world. Pat would canvass the neighborhood where Bonnie had lived but his search would be for friends and family of Bobby. Once again, A.J. pulled some strings and Pat would be accompanied by a professional. This time a private detective that A.J. had hired several times before.

Britt could assist Pat by following paper trails. Real estate that had been sold, forwarding addresses, payroll records, even IRS returns. It seemed A.J. had no limit to his resources.

In the meantime, they would meet three times each week to compile the data gathered and to alter their plans according to the progress being made.

9.

Bonnie had received two letters from A.J. They were continuing the search the letters had said, but the progress had been minimal. A.J. needed to visit with her again and to try hypnosis once more. Would she be available on the thirteenth of next month? She had laughed when she read the date. How could she know? Certainly she would be available, but dates were meaningless. She wrote a reply indicating her willingness to be of help then decided to visit the entrance tunnel gate every day till the mailbox lamp glowed.

Nineteen days later, as tracked by the number of stones she placed in a bowl, the lamp was lit.

The note inside the mailbox read, "Tomorrow at noon, Mr. Ripplestone will be arriving for a consultation."

She wondered if Mr. Ripplestone would be the elder or the young man that was close to her own age.

She and David, once again, sat in the sand waiting.

This time she was not overly concerned with the visit. She had reconciled her feelings of anxiety and had become convinced that she would not have to leave David and Lee. By the time this was over, she would be an old woman, David would be long dead and her son would be a fine grown man.

She was lost in these thoughts when the beacon over the tunnel entrance began its rude flashing.

They immediately stood and embraced. "I'll wait right here," David said. "Don't forget to ask about medicine. Especially penicillin."

The voice of the guards interrupted them and she turned to go.

"Bonnie, it's good to see you again," A.J. said. "Are you well?"

"Yeah. I mean, Yes. I'm okay, but there's others who aren't. Is it possible for you to send us medicine? We need penicillin desperately, and aspirin, and anything else you can get."

"Bonnie," A.J. said. "Bonnie, Bonnie, Bonnie. We had to get special permission just to send letters. I really don't think it will be possible..." He could see the disappointment in her eyes. "I'll see what I can do," he said. "But first, there's business we have to take care of." He squeezed her hands in his own.

"This gentleman is Doctor Andrew Hickey. He's a police officer and a psychologist. He specializes in hypnosis and has agreed to help me help you."

"Hello Doctor," she said shyly.

They repeated the exercise they had conducted last time.

They talked and they walked, walked and talked. Finally, A.J. suggested they rest awhile in the same day room they had been in on his last visit.

When they were seated, Bonnie asked if it were necessary to do all the talking before the hypnosis.

"Not really," the doctor said with a smile, "but it helps me to get to know you a little and that makes my job easier."

"Well, I'd like to start. I don't like to be away from my son."

Jack Radtke

"You have a son? Tell me about him," Hickey said.

The hypnosis session was already under way, but Bonnie didn't realize it.

As she relaxed to a greater extent, Hickey asked about she and Leroy arriving in Detroit. What had they done next? When did they find the house that they had rented? How was the pregnancy going?

These general questions led in small increments toward the date the two men were interested in exploring.

"And on that morning, what time did you awaken?" he said.

"Four twenty."

"Was that an unusual time to awaken?"

"Yes. I was sick. And I was bleeding"

"When did Leroy get up?" the doctor said.

"I don't know. He was already gone to work at the tire yard."

She was doubled over, clutching at her abdomen.

"You can remember all the details of that morning, but you are feeling no discomfort. In fact, you feel refreshed."

Bonnie raised her head and looked directly forward as if there were no one else in the room. Her hands moved to her lap in a relaxed position. "That's better," the doctor said. "What did you do when you got out of bed?"

"I threw up." She looked distastefully down and to her left. "Then I washed, checked the bleeding. I'm scared. Got to change the bedding." Bonnie's hands were working in her lap.

"Please go on."

180

"I want my mom. No answer. I'll go to a doctor. Just a couple more hours." She began rocking back and forth on the chair.

"Bonnie," the doctor said. "Two hours have passed. What are you doing now?"

"Bus. Going to see doctor."

They were recording the session, but A.J. was taking furious notes, anyhow. Sometimes he scribbled a hurried question for the doctor. The one he showed Hickey now read, "Doctor's name?"

The session lasted nearly six hours. Bonnie had never been to the store that had been held up. She was not in possession of any hand gun on that day. At A.J.'s prompting, Hickey asked her for directions to the store. She didn't know where the store was nor how to get to the intersection they described. She had access to no car. Her only transportation had been by bus. The visit to the doctor's office had consumed most of the day, with Bonnie lying on a cot in a back room till well after four in the afternoon.

A.J. was sure that a trial run on a bus from the doctor's office to the store would show that she couldn't possibly have been at the store at the time the crime occurred. Now, all A.J. wanted to do was rush to Detroit to verify by the doctor's records that Bonnie had been in to see him on that day. He only hoped that the doctor had kept decent records.

10.

A.J. and Pat left the doctor's office after finding the doctor wasn't in and wasn't expected until the next morning. They discovered they had to walk only one block to a bus stop. A.J. encouraged Pat to push his wheelchair quickly. They wanted to prove that there wasn't enough time for Bonnie to make the trip that they were duplicating. A.J. noted the time and wrote it in his notebook.

They waited forty minutes for a bus. A.J. made a note to subtract forty minutes from the total time. She could have been lucky and caught a bus immediately.

They told the driver their destination and asked about transfers. Pat sat on the seat immediately behind the driver. "Is the bus always this late?" he said.

"This time of night, yeah. Earlier in the day we do okay, though. Rush hour."

"How often does a bus come by?"

"Once an hour." The driver looked as though he was tiring of the questions.

"Just one more. If a pregnant woman got on the bus and then puked on your feet would you be able to remember her?"

"Damn right. Happened twice. Once last year. After she finally got situated, didn't go a half mile and she started screaming bloody murder. Had the baby right back there in the fourth row."

"What about the other time?"

"Named the kid after me. Alphonse. That's me. Alphonse Brown." The driver was grinning from ear to ear.

"That's nice. What about the other woman? When did that happen?"

A sour look crossed the driver's face. "I don't know. Long time ago. Maybe eight, ten years. No baby that time."

"What was it about that woman that makes you remember her?" Pat said.

"What!? You got to be kidding me, right? Puke. A woman pukes all over you, you going to remember. Believe me. You'll take that to the grave with you." He started laughing at the memory.

"That doesn't seem very funny to me."

"Oh, I was just remembering the look on her face. I think she was more surprised than I was."

"You remember her face?" Pat said. "Just a minute." He quickly moved to the rear of the bus where A.J. had parked his chair.

"A.J., where's that picture of Bonnie? I can't believe it. This is the same bus driver that drove Bonnie that day and he remembers her."

A.J. dug in his battered case and came up with two pictures. One taken in high school and one he had taken on the island. As Pat moved back toward the front of the bus, A.J. followed.

"Here," Pat said, thrusting the pictures in front of the man's face. "Is this her?"

Alphonse brushed Pat's hand away. "Can't you see I'm driving? And your friend, there, has to move back to the handicapped area. Can't be blocking the aisle."

A.J. was swearing under his breath but he managed to get out of his chair and sit on the seat to the right of

183

the driver in the first row. He faced sideways in the bus.

Pat folded the chair and placed it next to A.J.

When the driver stopped at the next traffic light, Pat was quick to show him Bonnie's picture again.

"Nope. That's not her." He pushed the picture back toward Pat.

"How about this one," Pat said. He was holding his breath.

Alphonse studied the older photograph for a minute then glanced up at the traffic light. It turned green. Still holding the photograph, he began to drive away. After he crossed the intersection, he checked his mirrors then turned the photo over in his hands and looked at it again.

Pat stole a look at A.J. who was staring so intently at the driver that he didn't even notice Pat looking his way.

The driver glanced between the picture and the road several times in succession then pulled over at a bus stop to pick up the next passenger. He watched the passenger board and made sure the correct token was placed in the coin machine. As the token tinkled in the bottom of the machine, he glanced in his left mirror then pulled from the curb, neatly cutting off an approaching car. "If it's not the same girl then it's her twin sister," Alphonse said.

Pat's head snapped down as if it had been held up by wires which had just broken. A.J.'s face broke into a creased smile.

"Young fellow," A.J. said, "I think I'd like to buy you a dinner. When do you get off work?"

Alphonse looked at A.J. suspiciously. "What's this about? Who are you guys?"

"Tell him, Pat. I think I just want to enjoy the ride."

Pat and A.J. temporarily abandoned their timed ride to the party store and continued with this bus till it reached the end of the line. They took advantage of the time to explain the circumstances surrounding their search and what Bonnie had been convicted of. They also asked Alphonse if he had remembered where Bonnie had gotten off the bus and if he had ever seen her again. The answer was no to both questions.

They ate in a small restaurant where the food was good but the menu was limited. They arranged for Alphonse to visit A.J.'s temporary office the following Saturday to give his statement, and recorded the conversation they had in the diner, as well. Alphonse agreed to testify if needed but required that they pay his wages if he had to lose any time from work. A.J. assured him that it would cost him nothing but his time and that they would even pay any out-of-pocket expenses. They encouraged him to make notes of anything else he might remember about the girl or the events of that trip. A.J. said he would send a cab to pick him up on Saturday.

They watched Alphonse walk out to an arriving bus and trade places with the incoming driver. A.J. shook his head. "Phenomenal," he said. "Purely phenomenal."

They called for a cab to take them back to A.J.'s place. They would try another timed run tomorrow.

11.

After the thrill of confirming with the doctor that Bonnie had been there on the day and time that she had remembered under hypnosis they made another run to the party store. This time in Pat's newly repaired car and during the middle of the day.

A.J. reasoned that if the bus trip proved too lengthy someone might opine that she had access to a car so he insisted on driving by car without benefit of rush hour traffic as well as taking a bus trip at the time of day when she supposedly left the doctor's office. The doctor had been unable to confirm the time of her departure, only that she had rested at his office for some time before departing. He thought it was shortly before his last patient when she left which would have been about five o'clock, but he couldn't swear to it.

The trip by car took thirty eight minutes. If she had left at five, she would have arrived at the store at five thirty eight. Allow a maximum of ten minutes for her to get her nerve up and enter the store and the crime would have been committed at twelve before six. The security tape had shown the hold-up beginning at six oh one. Thirteen minutes. "Damn," A.J. said quietly.

While they drove back to the doctor's office, A.J. was deep in thought. "Pat, first thing tomorrow, call city hall and see if you can find out if there was any construction going on, check the papers to see if there were any accidents or anything else which might slow traffic."

"A.J., tomorrow? I've got a deadline coming. I've got to get my thesis done and in to the printer to have it bound. I need a break, here."

A.J. smiled. "Whine, whine, whine. Okay, I'll have Britt do some digging. Are you done with the edited version?"

"Just came back yesterday. I took a quick glance at it. Having the editor go over the revisions wasn't nearly as painful as the first edit. I should be able to knock it out in a couple of days, then on to binding, mail it in, hold my breath and wait."

"You'll be all right," A.J. said. "I've read a few of those monsters in my day and yours is pretty good." He slapped Pat's knee. "Have you a date yet to take the Commission's bar exam?"

"No. Thought I'd wait to make sure I can put the 'C.C.' behind the J.D."

"Mmm. Better safe than sorry, huh?" A.J. looked amused. "Well, it's nearly five. Let's get out by that bus stop."

The bus was thirty one minutes late. Alphonse wasn't driving.

A.J. pointed up ahead. "This is where she would get off if she were going straight home."

Three stops later, they got off the bus, hurried across the street and stood at the next stop waiting for the bus that would take them on the next leg of their trip. "Notice that we're heading in the wrong direction from Bonnie's home. If she did this, there would have had to have been considerable thought put into it. It's not like she would have picked the party store at random. If you noticed, we've passed several other stores which would have been just as likely a target, if it were a spur of the moment thing."

The second bus arrived after only a seven minute wait.

Two miles later they got off. "From here, we have to walk several blocks," A.J. said. "Remember now, she had just come from a doctor's office, wasn't feeling well, even vomited on the bus driver. Now we need to believe she had the strength to walk these next blocks to rob a store."

Pat pushed A.J. at a fairly fast pace. "Can you imagine a sick pregnant woman walking at this speed?" Pat said. "Better have Britt check the temperature that day, as well. If it was a hot day, she would be walking slower."

They stopped at a pay phone bolted to the party store wall next to the entrance and called for a cab. A.J. was looking at his watch and beaming. "By now, the deed was done and ambulances were already on their way."

In the back of the cab A.J. was making plans. "You go ahead and take care of your doctorate. Britt and I will still follow up some of these loose ends, and I surely would like to find something on Bobby and that gun, then the three of us will begin to compile everything we've got into some kind of order. I think we're close to filing for an appeal hearing."

12.

Pat was just returning from approving the proofs of his manuscript prior to printing and binding. There was a cop car in front of his building and a biker leaning in the passenger window. As Pat got closer he thought, Knuckles. I can't do this again.

Pat pulled to the curb behind the police cruiser.

Knuckles glanced his way, spoke again to the occupant of the car then slapped the roof of the cruiser and joined Pat as he was getting out of his car.

"Padre." Knuckles swept him off his feet into a bear hug. "You clean up nice. Got a beer for an old buddy?"

"What do you want, Knuckles. I'm not going back out there with you again."

Knuckles laughed loudly and slapped Pat on the back.

"Just a progress report," he said. "Basil came through. C'mon. Let's get a beer." Knuckles led the way to Pat's apartment.

Suddenly, Pat was happy to see the man and thought if he really had to, he would go out with Knuckles maybe one more time.

Knuckles twisted the top off two bottles of red beer.

"It's probably not what you were hoping for, but it's a damn sight better than what I thought he'd find."

"What? Out with it."

"Old Basil found, not one, not two, but three buddies of old Bobby. Now they're not real friendly with cops and they don't have much use for lawyers, either, but when Basil told them you'd probably pop some cash for their trouble they got real friendly."

"Wait a minute. How'd they know I was a lawyer?"

"They don't. But Basil does. He's working under cover. So. Anyhow, two of the guys knew Bobby and they'll say under oath that they knew him, he was a scuzzball, and he regularly bought and sold guns, mostly hot. The third guy says he was tight with Bobby. Still misses him, the poor bastard.

"Anyhow, he don't know if Bobby did the job on your party store. Or if he does, he ain't saying. What he does say, though, is that Bobby regularly held up mom and pop stores, especially the all-night type of store, and bragged about shooting any clerk that gave him lip." Knuckles looked pleased with himself and leaned his head back and drained his beer.

"Well, the part about selling guns is good stuff, but it was a woman, a pregnant woman, that they caught on security tape, so I don't think it was Bobby that shot the clerk in this case."

"Let me finish, man," Knuckles said. "When Bobby went in, if it wasn't like three or four in the morning, he always wore a disguise. Blond wigs and a dress... sometimes brown or red wigs. And he was baby-faced, so he could probably pull it off.

"Basil says that the guy who was tight with him told him Bobby was a little short fat guy. Lotta guts but no brains and no muscles.

"Now the way I see it, it's not proof, but it might cause reasonable doubt, if that's good enough for you."

Knuckles pulled another beer from the refrigerator. "Oh yeah. One more thing. Basil says that the only job Bobby ever had besides doing stores was at a scrap tire place. But that's probably a dead end. Those places don't keep employment records. They pay cash and even if you could track the place down, they'd never admit that they had ever hired him. No records, no taxes." Knuckles winked, pulled a stained envelope from his back pocket and said, "I gotta go. Here's Basil's report, complete with names and addresses, or at least hangouts."

Pat was holding the report in his left hand, reaching for the phone with his right and thought, Knuckles, you sweet, sweet man.

After Alphonse left the law offices on Saturday afternoon, the three of them, A.J., Pat, and Britt, drove to Joe Muir's for a celebratory dinner.

A.J. held up his glass. "A toast," he said, "to perhaps the finest investigation team ever fielded on behalf of the Capital Crimes Commission."

They enjoyed their seafood dinner and talked at length about putting their case in order. Best estimate to a court date was six months.

"I believe," Britt said, "that we owe a certain young lady a letter."

13.

"Oh my god," Bonnie whispered.

"What is it? What's happened?" David saw mixed emotions on his wife's face.

"They've filed for an appeal. They think... Wait. They think they can show I'm innocent. They say. umm, just a minute. All circumstantial. Timing not right. Found friends of man who robbed store. Jesus, I don't know. Here, you read it." She thrust the letter at David.

David read slowly and looked up twice to look at Bonnie.

She was softly crying. David couldn't tell if it was happiness or fear. Her expression was unreadable. The third time he looked up, she wasn't there.

He found her outside their home, holding Lee. Tears were still cascading down her cheeks.

"What is it, Bonnie? Why the tears?" He held her with his right arm across her shoulders and with his left hand wiped her face.

"Did they say anything about the penicillin?"

"No. With news like this, they probably forgot all about it. Is that what you're concerned with?"

"Oh, David. If they're right, I'll have to leave you. I couldn't... I can't..." She began sobbing.

"Bonnie, Bonnie. You don't deserve to be here. You don't... Bonnie, look at me. I'm an old man. I'll probably die soon. Look. Look here." He pushed the letter in front of her. "It says it may take two years or more to complete the appeal. By then, who knows? I'll probably be gone. You deserve a better life than this. Take this opportunity, go home. Find a good man your own age. Someone who can give you what I cannot."

They sat in the sand yard long after the sun went down, wrapped in each other's arms. That night they made love, Bonnie trying desperately to determine how to hold her family together and David beginning to realize the end was nearing.

For the next two months, Bonnie wandered the island, seeing it as if for the first time. She tried to memorize the faces of friends, the shape of the shoreline, the smell of the sea breezes. Nearly every time she watched Lee playing, a tear would come to her eye. He frequently asked what was wrong with her and she always replied, "You give me so much joy, I can't help but cry when I see you." Then she would give him a big smile and send him back with his friends.

David continued to assure her he was dying, using the bittersweet logic that he was the oldest man on Regenesis and that he surely wouldn't last much longer.

"You have a strange way of comforting me," she would say. And yet, she was comforted. Not because she thought he might die soon, but because he was so sincere in wishing a better life for her. She hoped he wouldn't do anything to shorten their time together.

Another letter arrived. Hearings had started. Judges had been petitioned, their case had been laid out. An appeal, unlike the original trial, required a jury and one would soon be selected. Their original estimate of two years or more had been pessimistic. They now estimated a mere six months. Things were proceeding more quickly than they had originally thought. She should prepare for her return.

BOOK THREE

Jack Radtke

1.

A.J., Pat and Britt were gathered in A.J.'s hotel room.

The discussion was whether to have A.J. make all presentations or to have Pat assist. Having been awarded his doctorate degree and having taken the Commission's bar exam, but not yet notified if he had passed, he was still entitled to represent Bonnie as an assistant. They were merely deciding if it were in her best interests to do so.

Britt, although she had passed the Michigan bar exam, had not yet completed her education and therefore was not eligible to speak. She could, however, assist the team and would be in the courtroom for the entire process, save those times she might be called upon to run errands for the lead attorneys.

It had been decided that A.J. would be the primary speaker. If any of them had a sense that the jury was reacting coolly toward A.J., they would, at any time, switch to Pat.

The day had been a long one. The third in a row in which they argued before the judge the merits of allowing Bonnie to be released in A.J.'s custody. The prosecutor seemed outraged at the suggestion that a convicted criminal be free, or perhaps he was merely an excellent actor. The judge had promised a decision tomorrow. If A.J. lost, Bonnie would be lodged in the Bay County Jail for the duration of the trial.

"She's due in on Saturday," A.J. said. "If she remains free, I'd like all of us to meet her at the airport and either ride with the Marshall or at least escort them. When they arrive at the jail, one of us needs to arrange for an immediate attorney-client consultation, just to keep her from being processed. Once they start that, it will take at least three days to get her out again. If I can get the judge to intervene before the process begins, it's likely we'll be able to walk out of there with her in tow."

"Britt and I can handle the delaying tactics," Pat said.

They were all quiet again as they continued to read their game plan and review the prosecutor's likely attack. A.J. seemed to be comfortable in this exercise while both Pat and Britt were fidgeting in their chairs. A.J. looked up at them and half smiled.

"Let's have a little change," A.J. said. "Where's that list of jurors?"

Pat leaned across the bed and rifled through a stack of paper on the far side. "Here."

"Okay. Britt, dim the lights." A.J. moved his wheel chair so he could more comfortably see the blank wall on which the first juror's image would soon be displayed.

There was a flash of bright light when Britt punched the button to make the mechanism advance. "Sandra Dow. Twenty eight, married, two children, employed as a telemarketing salesperson. Works out of her home four days a week and visits her office on Fridays. Your reactions?" A.J. said.

"Airhead," Pat said. "She'll go with the majority."

"I don't think so," Britt said. "She gives that impression but I'll bet there's more between the ears than meets the eye. She works at home and is apparently successful enough to keep her job so she must have some discipline and is probably self motivated."

"Look at her hair. That 'just out of the shower' look went out years ago. And she dresses like a teenager. Always smiling. I'll bet her friends describe her as 'bubbly and vivacious.' I still say she's an airhead." Pat was smiling smugly.

"Next," A.J. said. That would be the extent of his input through the next fourteen photos. He wasn't interested in his own opinion.

The show lasted till after midnight and they each went to their own rooms. As they entered the late July humid night air, Pat said, "I never would have believed that A.J. would have this much stamina. Before the trial... Hell, in all the time I've known him, it was nap in the afternoon, go to bed before the sun was down and up at four."

"Well," Britt said as she reached the door to her room, "he'll be up at four, that's for sure. The question is, will we?" She winked a good night to Pat and disappeared inside.

A.J. had made arrangements with the judge to pick up Bonnie without assistance of the U.S. Marshall's office. He was to bring her directly to the judge's chambers so that the judge might impress upon her the situation she was in, the responsibility A.J. had accepted on her behalf, and what the penalties would be, should she decide to not cooperate.

After the meeting with the judge, A.J. and Bonnie rode by taxi to the motel. "You've waited a long time for this," A.J. said. "You don't seem very excited. Nervous?"

"No. A little scared, maybe, but mostly I miss Lee and David."

"Well, there's nothing to be scared of. I have a good feeling about this case." He patted her knee.

"That's mostly what I'm scared of."

They made the rest of the trip in silence, A.J. contemplating what she had said and watching her out of the corner of his eye.

When they had all met in A.J.'s room, Britt volunteered to take Bonnie shopping for some decent clothes to wear. They bought several suits that flattered her for court appearances and several changes of casual clothes, as well. Shoes were a problem. Her feet, unaccustomed to footwear, were now difficult to fit properly.

When they returned, Bonnie said she was tired and would like to rest. They agreed to meet later in A.J.'s room.

When the attorneys were alone, Britt said, "I don't think I've ever seen such strange reactions before. Bonnie would come out of a fitting room with her new clothes, and the look on her face was a cross between sadness, despair, joy, excitement, fear... I don't know, exactly. It was like all human emotion being displayed at once."

"When I told her I felt pretty good about her case," A.J. said, "she told me that is what she was afraid of." He contemplated the door through which Bonnie had walked moments earlier. "I hope we haven't made a mistake."

"Mistake?" Pat said. "Of course not. She's innocent. You're not having second thoughts, are you?" He looked from A.J. to Britt and back.

"No. I don't mean her innocence. I'm wondering if we made a mistake even taking the case, regardless of innocence."

After a short silence, Britt said, "I've heard of things like this. You know, some guy that spends nearly his whole life in prison then gets released only to find he doesn't like the world he sees and wants to go back inside. Commits some bonehead crime just to get thrown back in. Do you think that's what we've got here?" She looked to Pat for an answer.

"Perhaps, but unlikely. She's only been away a comparatively short time. What? Eight years? I think it's something else."

"I agree," A.J. said. "But I'll be damned if I know what. And we don't have time to figure out new puzzles right now. Opening statements are Monday morning. We've only got the rest of today and tomorrow to get her prepared and we've a lot of ground to cover."

"But her attitude is important, A.J.," Pat said. "We need to get to the bottom of this."

"Okay, okay. Britt, how did you hit it off? Think she would open up to you?"

"Maybe. But we don't exactly have time to develop an intimate friendship."

"Then put it in high gear. Tonight and tomorrow we'll take a break every two hours. You take her out of here and talk to her. Find out what's going on in her heart, or mind, or wherever the problem is. By the time we get to court on Monday, I want to see a

201

wholesome, healthy, sound-minded young woman sitting next to me."

2.

The court room was in the same Bay City Federal Building that housed the court Bonnie had been sentenced in eight years previously. The room was a different one, but the decor was almost identical to the one she remembered. Tall ceilings, fancy wainscoting, impressive oil paintings of long dead judges, the peculiar smell of aged oak and stale air.

The air conditioner whirred but the air was still stale and already it was becoming warm. Her new clothes felt stiff and uncomfortable and her feet were sore. She kicked off her shoes under the table.

On a raised platform in front of her were three fancy oak desks, joined together. To her right was the prosecutor's table. He was a tall, serious looking man, and he wore half spectacles on the tip of his nose. At the moment, he was arranging stacks of paper before him. There were six new pencils on the table, as well.

On the far right of the room were the jurors. They were the only ones who sat in comfortable looking chairs. She would have liked to look more closely at the individuals seated there, but every time she glanced in their direction, she found they were openly staring at her and it made her uncomfortable.

She turned to look over her shoulder. The spectator area was empty. That is, empty except for Britt. She was nice, Bonnie thought. And there, in the back, were two men. She didn't know who they were.

She heard a shout and turned in time to see that everyone was standing, so she stood, too. The judge was entering.

He was a little man with white hair. His hair was too long and so was his black robe. She half smiled when she noticed the robe dragging on the floor.

The judge sat at the middle desk and motioned for everyone else to sit. He arranged some papers, removed his glasses and cleaned them on the sleeve of his robe, while he looked at her from under bushy eyebrows. The clerk, probably the same man who had yelled earlier, was yelling again. Bonnie didn't catch the words but she had the sense that he was saying the court had to come to order and he gave the name of the judge, but she didn't catch that either. Suddenly things were happening too fast.

She looked to her right. Mr. Ripplestone sat next to her and seemed completely relaxed. Next to him was Pat. Pat sat on the edge of his chair and leaned forward with his forearms on the table.

The judge tapped the microphone with a fingernail. The sharp clicking sound echoed in the room. "Ladies and Gentlemen of the jury. I would like to take a few moments to explain the proceedings before you.

"You'll notice the court is nearly empty. That's because this is a capital crimes appeal case. By statute, these proceedings are closed to the public. You may correctly infer that since the public is not invited, everything you may see or hear is not for publication, now or in the future. In plain English, I have issued a gag order.

"Capital crimes are handled differently than any you may be accustomed to. A panel of three judges hear capital crimes cases, not a jury. Their decision is reached in only three or four days, in most cases.

"It is indeed, rare, to have before us, a defendant convicted of a capital crime who has successfully been granted an appeal.

"We will hear this case, you the jurors, and I. There is more latitude given to the opposing attorneys and as a result you may hear things that surprise you. Trust me to ensure that the proceedings are carried out with appropriate decorum."

He went on for some time. At first, Bonnie was intensely interested in the judge's remarks but found she was soon bored and began to look at the jurors. They were rapt with attention to the judge and none looked her way.

There were twelve of them in the juror's box and three more sitting just outside the box. They didn't seem so hostile now. Perhaps it was only curiosity that led them to stare at her before. Much as she felt about them.

The silence caused Bonnie to be aware of the judge once again. When she looked his way, he was cleaning his glasses again. He looked up. "Who stands before this court?" he said.

"May it please the court, Daniel J. Page, P-A-G-E, for the Capital Crimes Commission."

"Let the record show that Daniel J. Page represents the Capital Crimes Commission," the judge said. "And representing the defendant?"

A.J. stood, leaning heavily on the table. "Please," the judge said, "you may remain seated."

"Thank you, your honor, but as long as I am able..."

"Very well," the judge said.

"May it please the court, Albert J. Ripplestone, R-I-P-P-L-E-S-T-O-N-E, and Mr. Patrick S. Ripplestone, same spelling, for the defense."

A.J. and Pat both sat while the judge ordered that they be recognized for the record.

He turned to the prosecution table. "Mr. Page, you may begin. Try to limit your comments to one hour."

Bonnie swallowed hard and reached for the glass of water in front of her as she watched the tall man approach the jury box.

Page stood in front of the jury, arms crossed, a scowl on his face. Finally he spoke. "Ladies and gentlemen. Let me thank you for giving of your time. I know you are all busy and this is an imposition. And I apologize for my demeanor. I don't mean to be abrupt with you." His face seemed stern as he panned across the jurors. "I am simply hard pressed to understand why this panel has been gathered in the first place.

"The woman before you, Bonnie White," he paused and lifted his arm toward Bonnie, "has been convicted of a double murder, her husband and her own child. For this, she has been sentenced. Now, she stands before you, appealing this decision. And on what grounds, you may ask.

"Was there a catastrophic breakdown of our legal system? No. There was not. Has new evidence been discovered? No. There has not. What then? What brings you from your busy lives to this courtroom?

"I'll tell you. She would have you believe that the problem lies with her defense attorney. He was not zealous enough. The facts were there, she says, but her defense attorney did not present them adequately. Witnesses were not brought forward."

Page stopped speaking for a moment while he paced in front of the paneled jurors, seeming to will his anger out of his voice. When he spoke again, he was calm, his voice softer, the scowl gone.

"We will show you a young woman, whose marriage was falling apart, a woman who was desperate for love and for those things her unemployed husband could not provide, a woman, who in the end felt compelled to shoot and kill, not only her husband but her baby daughter as well."

Page walked to his table and pulled an object from a cardboard box. Turning to face the jury, he held up a small handgun. "We will show that this woman used this gun to commit at least one other crime in which she shot a store attendant." Page's voice was rising. "She later used this same gun, and forensic tests will verify this, she used this same gun to kill her husband," at which Page gripped the gun with both hands and pointed it toward an imaginary target, "and to kill her own baby." He finished with sadness in his voice and he mimicked a mother holding a baby to her breast with his left arm while the gun in his right hand pointed at the imaginary baby's head.

Bonnie had to look away for fear she would begin crying.

She tried to take the advice that A.J. had given yesterday. Just ignore the proceedings while the prosecutor is speaking and maintain a bland expression. Stare at the table, but don't make eye contact with the jurors.

Jack Radtke

Page had taken slightly more than the allotted hour to make his presentation. When he had finished, the judge recessed for two hours for lunch. He admonished the jury to speak to no one about the trial and not to discuss it among themselves.

As A.J., Pat and Bonnie walked toward the rear of the courtroom, Bonnie said, "He's good, isn't he?"

3.

A.J. sat before the jurors. He gave them a few moments to become accustomed to his wheelchair. He didn't want their attention to be diverted by the appliance once he began to speak and so allowed time for them to become comfortable.

When he raised his eyes to meet those of the jurors he was softly smiling. He greeted them with a gentle "Good afternoon." He pivoted his chair to the right and wheeled six feet along the edge of the jury box and spun the chair around to face them. He slapped the arm of the chair with his right hand. The noise echoed in the silent court.

"They tell me a good speaker never begins by apologizing. But I must. I apologize for this contraption." He slapped the arm again for emphasis. "It prevents me from gesturing as effectively as I had in my youth. It prevents me from making eye contact with each of you. But..." A.J. paused for a long moment. "I trust it will not prevent you from hearing and recognizing the truth of what will be said before you over these next days and weeks."

Every eye in the court was on him as he wheeled to the opposite end of the jury box. He spun again, more slowly this time.

"I am old. Hence this contraption." He looked at each of them individually. "Yes. I am old. I have practiced law nearly my whole life as an agent for the Capital Crimes Commission. A long time." With his right hand he pushed the right wheel back and forth giving his whole body a contemplative bearing. "This

209

is likely to be my last case. I would not waste it with a defendant who was not deserving nor one who was anything less than completely innocent."

Pat was busy making notes on the reactions of individual jurors to A.J.'s words and his gestures.

"We have an opportunity to make right a decision that was wrong. Terribly wrong. We can release this young woman who so desperately deserves to be released. Listen for a few moments.

"Mr. Page would have you believe this is a frivolous case. One without merit. Not worthy of your time."

The implication was clear. If the case was worthy of this old man's time, of the time he would spend on the last case of his career, it was surely worth their time.

"No new evidence, he says. The original defense attorney acted with appropriate zeal on behalf of Bonnie White." A.J. pointed toward Bonnie and waited while each juror looked her way then looked back to him again. "We will show that Ms. White spoke the truth and provided all the information for her defense to act upon. That defense was unable or unwilling to verify the facts as she gave them. Now, over eight years later, this old man," A.J. slapped his wheelchair again, "and my two associates, one barely out of law school and one still attending, were able to verify her story." He paused for a moment. "To find witnesses, to gather affidavits, to clearly find the truth.

"Mr. Page would have us believe that her zealous defense attorney, only weeks after her arrest, was unable to discover any corroborating data."

A.J. slowly wheeled his chair toward the defense table but stopped halfway and spun slowly about.

"I'll tell you now, and prove to you through these proceedings, what really happened."

He told in detail, and with some passion, how Bonnie had grown up, met her husband, got off to a shaky start, and moved to a strange and potentially dangerous city. How they had struggled to survive, her husband working long hours, living in the worst possible conditions. He described the attitudes of the neighbors. The distrust toward strangers. The employer refusing to admit that Leroy was an employee.

Through all of this, his voice worked through its full range. One moment softly pleading for understanding, the next shouting indignation.

At the close to his remarks he wheeled close to the jury box rail and looked directly into the eyes of a middle aged woman seated there. "Imagine," A.J. said in a low voice, "living in the worst that Detroit has to offer. Imagine a burglar entering the sanctity of your home, shooting your only child while you held her protectively in your arms. Imagine discovering you have just shot your own husband, the only man left in your world.

His voice rose as he wheeled backwards away from the rail. "Did we help her? No!" he shouted. His eyebrows furrowed deeply. We arrested her. We imprisoned her."

He waited a long moment. "Mr. Page asked if the system failed. It did not. The system is sound. It is people who fail. Even in the best of systems. Don't fail Bonnie White again."

A.J. waited so long before speaking again, the judge was on the verge of asking if he had completed his opening. The jurors had still not stopped watching him. One of them, a man, was wiping his eyes. Two of the women quietly let tears course down their cheeks. A.J. spun slowly toward his table.

"Thank you," the judge said. "Tomorrow morning at nine."

Someone shouted, "All rise." The jurors, now standing, still gazed toward A.J. Finally, they turned and filed from the room.

"Mr. Ripplestone," Page said, "You appear to be every bit as dramatic as I have been told. I hope the content of your case is equally impressive." Page turned and walked through the swinging gate of the bar.

A.J. showed no reaction to the encounter.

4.

"The Commission calls Detective Sergeant Wayne Albright."

The detective was sworn and climbed into the witness stand. He carried with him a manila folder with several papers neatly placed inside. The jurors were fidgeting in their chairs, trying to get comfortable.

"For the record, would you please give us your full name, including spelling." Page said.

The officer complied.

"You were the arresting officer?"

"Yes sir."

Page continued for some time, establishing that Albright had been in traffic control at the time and had responded to what he thought was a routine family disturbance complaint made by a neighbor of the White's. The complaint was for excessive noise, he told the court.

When he arrived at the scene, he was unable to gain entry by knocking on the door. From the interior he heard screaming and decided that perhaps a life was in peril. He drew his service revolver and opened the screen door. The inside door was open. There were no lights on in the building. Using his flashlight, he approached the bedroom, the room from which the noise emitted.

"And what did you find upon entering that room?" Page said.

"In the doorway of the room was a body. Male, Caucasian, early twenties."

"You said 'body'. Did you believe him to be dead?"

"Not at that time," the officer said. "I was distracted by screams coming from within the room."

"Please tell the court what happened next."

"I directed my light into the room. There was a woman on the floor, covered in blood. She was pointing a weapon at me and attempting to fire it. I dropped to one knee and pointed my service weapon at her, then realized the gun must have been empty. I identified myself as a police officer and demanded she lower the gun."

"And did she? Lower the gun, that is?"

"No sir. She threw it at me."

"And then, Detective? Please use your own words to describe the next events," Page said.

"She was hysterical. Still screaming. I stood and fumbled for a light switch. When the light went on I could see that she was covered in blood, as well. She was holding a baby but the baby looked dead. I used my portable radio to call for back-up. She wouldn't let me get near her, so I checked the man on the floor. He appeared to be dead. I kept talking to the woman and was finally able to get close enough to check the baby. The baby was also dead."

"Did the woman recover sufficiently to say anything to you?"

"The only thing she said was 'Oh my God, I killed him'. She kept saying it, over and over."

"What happened next?" Page said.

"She wouldn't let me take the baby, so I left them there on the floor. I handcuffed her left ankle to her right wrist, then I called in a probable homicide and secured the building."

"Do you see the woman in this courtroom?" Page said.

Before the detective could respond, A.J., not quite able to rise, said, "The defense concedes to the defendant being the woman in the scene just described." He lowered himself back into his wheelchair.

Page glanced at A.J. with raised brows. "I have no further questions, your honor."

The judge looked toward A.J. "Your witness, counselor."

A.J. wheeled himself from behind the table. "Just a few questions, your honor." He gazed at the detective as though contemplating what those questions might be. "Detective, you said the woman was pointing a gun toward you and trying to shoot you. Does this mean a shot was fired but she missed?"

"No sir."

"How then," A.J. said, "could you tell that she was trying to shoot you?"

"She was going like this." The detective demonstrated by holding an imaginary gun and pointing an index finger toward A.J. He jerked his hand, pointing emphatically at A.J. "With each jerk of her hand, I presumed she was pulling the trigger and anticipating a recoil."

A.J. turned to the recorder. Even though the entire proceeding was being video taped, the court recorder was still required to record what was being said, and the gesturing by the detective needed to be recorded, as well.   A.J. described for her the movements the detective had made.

He returned his attention back to the detective.

"Could it have been," A.J. said, "she was merely trying to give you the gun?"

"That was not my impression. No."

"You have testified that she was hysterical. In that frame of mind, would a gesture to relieve herself of this weapon be mistaken for attempted firing?" With this, A.J. mimicked the detective's gesture but his facial expression clearly said, 'take this disgusting thing away'.

"I don't think so. Her eyes. Her eyes had fear in them. She would have shot me if she could."

"This was before you identified yourself as a police officer?"

"Yes."

"So, she didn't know who you were and perhaps was shooting, or attempting to shoot, out of fear? A primal fear?"

"Yes sir. I think she was."

"No further questions, your honor."

The judge had, once again, removed his glasses and was cleaning them on his sleeve. "Redirect?"

"No further questions, your honor," Page said.

"Call your next witness."

Detective Warren Handy, retired, was called, sworn, and took the stand.

Page led the witness through the steps necessary to establish that at the time of the crime, he had been in charge of the investigation.

"At what point," Page said, "did Ms. White. Strike that. How long did the investigation take prior to charging Ms. White?"

"She was charged with open murder within two hours of my arrival."

"Upon what information or facts did you base that charge?"

"Her confession. It was pretty clear who had pulled the trigger."

"Is this her written statement?" Page said.

Handy looked over a two page document. "Yes sir."

Page introduced the document as evidence and labeled it as exhibit one and gave a copy to the clerk, one to A.J. and one to the judge. He returned to Handy.

"When the statement was signed, did that terminate the investigation? Was the case considered closed?"

"I had thought so. We took the statement from the defendant along with my report and the report of the responding officer to the district attorney. The D.A. wanted additional information regarding the child."

"And what information was deemed lacking?" Page said.

"The confession pertained only to the death of her husband. She denied having shot her child, so we needed to check that out."

"Do you recall the results of that portion of the investigation?" Page said.

"Yes sir. An autopsy was ordered on both bodies. Forensics showed the bullet that killed Mr. White and the bullet that killed the child had both been fired from the same handgun that Ms. White was holding when the responding officer arrived on the scene. We presented the lab reports, but several days later discovered we were still not finished with the case."

Handy leafed through some notes he held in his lap.

"We were ordered to run a routine search for other possible crimes committed with the same handgun," Handy said. "We determined that an unsolved shooting at a convenience store had involved the same weapon."

A.J. leaned toward Pat. "Pay dirt," he whispered.

"What, if anything," Page said, "was the significance of that finding."

"I didn't realize it at the time, but the events bumped the crime from a simple homicide to a double homicide to a Capital Crimes multiple homicide. You know, no longer a crime of passion."

"Objection," A.J. said. "Level of passion has not been established."

"Sustained," the judge said.

Page directed himself once more to Mr. Handy. "Had you formed any opinion, prior to your discovery of the convenience store shooting, of the frame of mind of the defendant at the time of the original crime. That is, at the time Mr. White had been shot?"

"Yes sir. I thought it was a simple family disturbance. I figured she'd plea bargain to manslaughter."

Clearly, Page had not expected this candid answer. He looked surprised, then his facial muscles worked to regain composure.

"Mr. Handy, was it routine for you to be called to a family disturbance that resulted in multiple homicide?"

"Happens more often than you'd think."

Handy had left the impression that due to the many, many times he had been involved in similar crimes, he was no longer shocked or even surprised at the various forms of human misery. It was clear that one body, two bodies, even three bodies were of minimal interest to him.

A.J. quickly scribbled a note and passed it to Pat.

"This helps," the note read, "skip the cross???"

Pat scribbled below it, "Need to show Handy's involvement after CC got involved." and passed the paper back to A.J.

Page was trying to recover. "Mr. Handy, it is safe to say that even though there sometimes occurs a crime of passion in the home resulting in death, that it is highly unusual to discover the same weapon being used in a crime wherein the perpetrator and the victim were strangers?"

"It's unusual that we discovered it to be true. We don't normally carry routine investigations to this extent and were just lucky to make the discovery."

"Okay," Page said. "Having made this discovery, were you able to show that the defendant was personally involved in the convenience store shooting?"

"Yes we were. We reviewed the evidence from that instance and discovered a security tape that revealed a young woman holding what appears to be the same gun on the clerk in that store."

"Can you testify with certainty that the girl in the tape and the defendant are one and the same?"

"It is my belief they are the same person."

Page introduced into evidence, two tapes. The original, untouched version and a digitally enhanced version. The enhanced version used a computer to enhance shadows and make clearer the original version which was of poor quality due to the same tape having been used over and over by the store's security system which continually looped the tape.

The court took a recess while technicians set up the necessary equipment to view the tapes. In thirty minutes, the court reconvened and the lights were dimmed. Three monitors had been set up. One for the benefit of the jury, one for the judge and one for the defense table.

The original untouched tape was played first.

Afterward, Page asked Handy to re-affirm that the girl on the tape and the defendant were, in his opinion, the same person.

"The defendant is older and slimmer now and the likeness isn't as dramatically the same as it was then, but they're the same person," Handy said.

They played the second tape. A.J. was surprised at how much the image on the tape appeared to be Bonnie. Had he seen that tape eight years ago, he would have probably sworn it was the same person, as well.

"May we approach?" A.J. said.

In deference to A.J.'s confinement to a wheelchair, the judge motioned them to the side of the bench where he met the three attorneys.

"I suspect," A.J. said, "counsel is prepared to bring witness after witness to testify as to the accuracy of the 'doctored' tape."

"I object!" Page said. "'Doctored, indeed.'"

"Sorry," A.J. said. "We merely wish to make a concession. Not to whose likeness may or may not be depicted, but to the accuracy of the technology. In the interest of time, we accept that the doctoring… excuse me," A.J. said with a smile, "the enhancements… were correctly and accurately done."

"I see some value in that," the judge said. He removed his glasses and was absently wiping them on his sleeve. "Counselor?"

Page smiled as if he had won a great victory. "I agree," he said.

They returned to their places.

"No further questions, your honor."

The judge looked at the clock hung at the rear of the courtroom and suggested they adjourn for the day. Both teams agreed.

They convened in A.J.'s room, the four of them, and discussed the events of that day. A.J. was encouraged. The witnesses produced so far had shown much less enthusiasm for a conviction than the jury probably expected. Page had brought up the convenience store which would allow them an opportunity to use it in their defense. If Page had overlooked that detail, the strongest part of their case would have gone up in smoke. The second witness, Handy, had subtly blown Page out of the water and A.J. argued that it might be the best plan not to cross examine that witness at all. Let the jury remember Mr. Handy with the impressions that Page had left with them.

Jack Radtke

Pat argued that Handy would be the ideal witness to pursue to show that the police had not been interviewed by either the original prosecutor or the defense attorney in preparation for that case. It would show sloppiness and a general lack of zeal. It would also be an opportunity to show that the police hadn't canvassed the neighborhood, hadn't determined if the timing was right for Bonnie to be there that day and at that time, or even pursued her story to determine if there had been any conflicts in fact.

5.

Court reconvened on Wednesday morning. Mr. Handy had re-taken the stand. A.J. was wheeling slowly toward him. Handy looked bored.

"Mr. Handy," A.J. said, "yesterday you testified to your activities during the investigation of the death of Mr. White. I don't recall. Did you give a deposition for use in that trial?"

"No sir."

"Were you asked for a deposition?"

"No sir."

"Were you interviewed by either the prosecution or by the defense?" A.J. was now facing the jury and with this question raised one eyebrow as if he couldn't believe what he was hearing.

"No sir, I wasn't. Except as I've already testified."

"Of course," A.J. said. "Did you volunteer to be of assistance to either of the attorneys?"

"No sir. We have hundreds of homicides to process each year. I was happy to put this one behind me."

"Process? Never mind. I'll withdraw the question."

A.J. put on an expression of disgust, then turned back toward Handy.

"What was your level of involvement after the Capital Crimes Commission determined this to be in their jurisdiction?"

"None, whatsoever."

"Does it strike you as unusual that neither party saw fit to speak to you about this... I mean, merely the

223

name of the Commission, Capital Crimes... doesn't that strike you that this crime was above and beyond the norm for criminal activity?"

"It was a clear cut case. There were no questions. She did it. She confessed."

"Did it strike you as being unusual that she would confess to shooting her husband, but strongly denied shooting her child, or later, denied shooting the store clerk?"

"No. Who can tell what goes through the minds of these people?"

"Perhaps the truth, Mr. Handy."

"Objection," Page said. "Is that a question?"

"I'll re-phrase, your honor," A.J. said.

"Mr. Handy," A.J. said, "did you, or to your knowledge, any member of the Detroit Police Department, attempt to verify any part of the story that Ms. White insisted was the truth?"

"Of course not."

A.J. spun his chair toward the defense table, facing the jury as he did so. "No, of course not," he said. "No further questions, your honor."

"Re-direct?"

"Yes, your honor," Page said.

Page stood, but did not approach the witness stand.

"Mr. Handy, in your many years as a police detective, have you ever been invited to testify or provide a deposition at a Capital Crimes Commission trial?"

"Only at this one."

"No further questions, your honor."

The trial continued in much the same tone over the next six weeks. Page brought before the jury every person known to have had a hand in the conviction of Bonnie White with much of the testimony based upon the belief that she was guilty prior to the trial. In each case, A.J. picked away at their credibility, showing the jury that having made the assumption of guilt, all involved found it very easy to not look for the truth.

If the jury retired now, after the prosecution rested, A.J. felt she would again be pronounced guilty, but at least this time, the jury would be out for several days considering reasonable doubt. He had accomplished that much, he believed.

It was a Wednesday. Court would reconvene on Monday.

It would be his turn. Time to turn the tables, if he could. The prosecutor, he suspected, was not prepared for the direct approach that A.J. had planned. The team would need these few days to rest and to prepare for battle.

6.

Monday morning found them seated in their customary positions in the courtroom. The judge had taken this opportunity to brief the jurors on what might be expected from the defense team. He explained that a Capital Crimes Commission appeals case allowed the defense team certain liberties which they may find unusual but to rest assured. He would not permit either the defense or the prosecution to encroach on the rules of his court. He removed his glasses and wiped them on his sleeve as he instructed A.J. to begin.

A.J. wheeled from behind the table and faced the judge.

"May it please the court, the defense wishes to begin by calling several witnesses, all of whom are important to the truth of this matter before us, but many of whom were unable to attend due to great distances and previous commitments."

The judge peered through his heavy brows at A.J. but said nothing.

"We have obtained depositions in these several instances and have video tapes we wish to share with the court."

"Objection, your honor," Page spat out. "The prosecution for the Commission has not had the opportunity to view these tapes."

"Your honor," A.J. said, "transcripts were provided to the prosecution and mention was made that videos had been recorded for use in the event that these parties may be unable to attend. Counsel has had ample opportunity to file motions to prevent."

The judge called for a side bar, then after a short conference announced to the jurors that he and the attorneys would retire to his chambers where they would view the videos and he would determine whether they would be allowed. He expected this exercise to take the better part of the morning.

At the judge's signal, the jury was led from the room as was Bonnie. The judge, the attorneys and Britt went to the judge's chambers. Britt loaded the first tape, adjusted the sound level and retired behind the others.

The exercise took only two hours and the judge had ruled against many of the scenes that he viewed as being too emotionally charged. The factual information was allowed and Britt was instructed to edit the tapes according to the footage markers that the judge had indicated.

It took Britt several hours to make the editing changes and the group met again at six that evening to review the tapes once more. Page continued to object but the judge was clear in his ruling and would not be swayed. Court would resume in the morning.

A.J. greeted the jurors and explained that they would be viewing several tapes which had been edited for content and that they should put as much value in what they saw and heard as if the witnesses were actually on the stand. He assured the jurors that the witnesses had been sworn prior to making the tapes.

Page objected. He reasoned that the value of the taped depositions were somewhat less than having the witness on the stand since he would be unable to cross examine them.

The judge pointed out, for the benefit of the jury, that a deposition is precisely the same as having a witness on the stand. When a witness makes a statement, that can be made in front of counsel for the prosecution and the defense, thereby allowing for as much cross examination as either side chooses. In some cases, if both parties are not present, as has occurred in these cases, a transcript is given to the absent attorney and if that attorney so chooses, he may arrange for a cross examination at any time prior to submitting the statement to the court. In this case, the prosecutor apparently felt a cross examination was not necessary. The judge looked pointedly toward Page.

"Please begin," the judge said to A.J.

A.J., with Britt's help, showed several tapes in sequence. First, Bonnie's mother describing Bonnie's early home life and how she had been abused by her father, but that she had grown to be a good girl who had never been in any trouble. This was followed by an interview with Bonnie's sister, Marie, who described Bonnie as her best friend. After Marie, the jury heard from two classmates of Bonnie's, both of whom testified that Bonnie had been unusually inactive in social affairs. Not that she was unpopular, she just seemed to prefer family over friends. The last tape featured Bonnie's mother-in-law, Mrs. White. She described the courtship between her son and Bonnie, how she never believed that Bonnie would intentionally hurt either her son, Leroy, or her grandchild. She went on for some time about their trip to Las Vegas to get married, the short honeymoon and the few letters she had received from the children when they were struggling to make ends meet in Detroit.

The jury would have time to contemplate Bonnie's personality during the two hour lunch break the judge had called.

Notably missing from the various tapes was any indication from the boys in Bonnie's class that may have indicated she was the class tease, and Britt had skillfully edited that portion of the tape which described Bonnie arriving at the White household after being thrown out of her own home by her father for becoming pregnant.

The end result depicted Bonnie as the girl next door but possibly a little more naive than the average teenage girl.

After lunch, A.J. called his first live witness. "The defense calls Clement Woods."

After Clem was sworn and had taken the stand, A.J. approached him and asked, "Did you know Leroy White?"

"Yes sir."

"Can you tell the court how you happened to meet?"

"Leroy worked for me. We met when he barged into my shop demanding a job. I hired him. Turned out to be my best worker."

"At Ms. White's previous trial, you did not testify. Was there a reason for this oversight?"

"A man from the prosecutor's office came by and asked me about Leroy. I told him I didn't know him and that he had never worked for me."

"You just said he was your best employee," A.J. said. "Why would you have denied that he worked for you?"

Clem looked down and squirmed in his chair. "My records weren't up to date. I might not have paid all the taxes I should have."

"Was Leroy considered a 'day laborer', one that was paid cash on a daily basis and no records kept of his employment?"

"Um, yeah. Yes. At least in the beginning. After he was there for a while, I made him a machine repairman and a foreman. I guess I just forgot to sign him up as a regular."

"To your knowledge, did Leroy own a gun?"

Clem was obviously relieved at the change in subject.

"Yes, at least two. One I sold him myself and a second one he bought later for his wife from another guy that sometimes worked for me."

"Were these legal guns? Registered?"

"No. The gun I sold him was clean. But Leroy didn't have a permit to buy or to carry, at least not that I know of."

"But he did carry, didn't he?" A.J. said.

"Yeah. Everybody did. We held them in the safe when they were working."

"Why would Leroy, or any of your other employees feel the need to carry weapons?"

"Object. Conjecture," Page said.

"Over-ruled. I'll allow it," the judge said.

"Bad neighborhood. Our building was full of bullet holes. But just getting to work and back home was dangerous, especially if you came in early or left late. All the guys carried."

A.J. was facing the jurors now. "Tell me about the second gun, the one he bought for Ms. White."

"A sissy gun. For women. I think it was a twenty two, maybe a twenty five."

"Who sold it to Leroy?"

"I don't remember."

"Could it have been Bobby Joe Smith?"

"Yeah, I think maybe it was. Yeah, Bobby."

"Did you know Bobby well?" A.J. said.

"No. Not very. He was half crazy. He only showed up when he needed some quick money to make a score. Drugs."

"Was Bobby into criminal activity? Do you have any knowledge of him using a weapon in the Commission of a crime?"

Page objected but before he had completed the syllables, the judge over-ruled him.

"I was never with him or nothing, but he used to brag about taking out anybody gave him a hard time. You know, he might have just been bullshi... Um, lying."

"You mean, he would shoot people just for the fun of it?"

"No, it wasn't like that. He said he'd hold up stores for some quick cash. If they gave him a hard time, sometimes he would shoot somebody, that's all. You know?"

"Yes," A.J. said. "I'm afraid I do know. One last question. Did Leroy tell you why he felt compelled to purchase a gun for his wife?"

"Yeah. He said she was terrified living where they lived, with him working the long hours and all. He felt she needed the protection. They'd been burglarized several times, once while she was home alone."

Page ineffectively cross examined Clem. It was clear to A.J. that Page didn't understand where they were going with this defense.

7.

A.J. brought in Clem's father to establish him as an eye witness to the sale of the weapon by Bobby to Leroy. It was a short exchange and Page didn't question the man.

The defense's next witness was a police officer that worked in the records department of the Detroit Police Department. He established that the White residence had placed seven burglary calls and six prowler calls during the three months prior to the shootings.

A.J. moved to a new subject. The search for Bobby.

They called Knuckles to the stand. His name was given to the recorder privately and he was introduced to the jury as an active duty undercover police officer. Pat questioned him.

"Officer," Pat said, "you recently accepted an assignment to find anyone that could shed some light on Bobby Joe Smith. Could you tell us about that search?"

"Yes sir. I had been informed that Mr. Smith had been fatally wounded in an aborted hold up attempt over eight years ago. I checked his records, found he had been arrested seventeen times, was incarcerated twice and hung around with biker gangs, but was not a member himself. I worked with members of the defense team and infiltrated several of the known hang-outs of these gangs and began spreading the word that we would like to meet any of Bobby's friends."

"What did you discover?" Pat said.

"Nothing that was a surprise. Those that knew of him pretty much echoed what his sheet had said. Small time, petty level, did crimes to feed his drug habit."

"So you were unable to find any close friends that could shed any light on Bobby Joe Smith's sale of a handgun to Leroy White?"

"Not personally, but I was able to make contact with another under cover police officer who has more experience in the group that we were searching. I had been out of circulation for a while and was being viewed with some suspicion, so I imposed on him to continue the search."

"Would it be safe to say," Pat said, "that Bobby Joe Smith was unsavory, dealt in drugs and guns, was likely to sell guns, and that those guns were likely stolen and had been used in previous crimes?"

Knuckles smiled. "That would suit him to a tee."

As Knuckles left the stand, Page stood and asked where, if anywhere, this line of thought was heading. He pointed out that Ms. White was on trial, not Bobby Joe Smith, or Smith's friends.

The judge looked toward Pat and then toward A.J. "I presume, counselors, that there is a point to this?"

"Yes, your honor. We will be showing conclusively that Bobby Joe Smith, and not Ms. White, was directly responsible for the shooting of the clerk that Ms. White has been accused of shooting."

"Very well. Please come to the point as quickly as is feasible. Proceed."

Pat called Basil to the stand and once again, special procedures were taken to ensure his true identity remained secure.

"Officer, you were asked to assist a fellow officer in the search for friends, associates, relatives of a Mr. Bobby Joe Smith. Please tell the court what you were able to discover."

It was a short testimony. Basil was able to recount discovering three friends of Bobby's but was prevented from disclosing what they had to say about their friend by repeated objections by Page. At a quick conference at the defense table, A.J. whispered, "Give it up. We'll have to call the bikers in."

Pat thanked Basil and declared that he had no further questions. Page looked triumphant. A.J. asked to approach the bench.

"Your honor, in light of the testimony previously given, or in this case, not given, we are compelled to call three other witnesses. It is vital to our case that they be heard, but it is our contention that they will refuse to testify. It may take some doing to convince them. Naturally, if we can convince them, we'll specify that they are hostile witnesses."

The judge looked to Page but Page remained aloof and had no comment.

"How much time will you need?" he asked A.J.

A.J. looked to Pat for a response. "It may take several days to find them and probably several more days to convince them, your honor. Perhaps a week?"

The judge said, "We will recess till Friday morning. Give the names to the Marshall. These punks will see how much power this court has. Convince them, my ass."

When they approached the Marshall, they gave him the names, as requested, but suggested he rely heavily on Basil to find the men.

In the end, Basil led Knuckles and several of Knuckle's 'friends' to a bar, pointed them out, and let Knuckle's party escort them away. Several blocks later, the Marshall took over.

On Friday, Pat resumed his questioning with the first of Bobby's friends. By the time he had finished with the third one, it was clear that Bobby was probably the shooter in the convenience store. To put the icing on the cake, Pat asked the third friend to view the security tape that the prosecutor had introduced into evidence. He only showed him the enhanced version.

"Holy shit! My man! That's Bobby. That's him."

The judge rapped his gavel twice. Clearly the judge was concerned that the young man's exuberance was about to get out of control.

"You're sure?" Pat said.

"Yeah, man. That be him. Hey! Can I have a copy of that tape?"

"No further questions," Pat said.

A.J. half stood from his wheelchair. "The defense makes a motion to commute the sentence of Ms. White as a matter of law. Without the presence of the crime witnessed on the video tape, Ms. White would not have been brought before the Capital Crimes Commission, and therefore her sentence, if not the entire trial, was out of scope."

Neither the jury nor Bonnie had any idea what had just happened. Confusion was apparent on the faces of the jury. A.J. did not turn to look at Bonnie.

The judge called for a side bar. "Gentlemen," the judge said, "this is a travesty. Had anyone the gumption to pursue these matters in the first place, we would not be here today. That young lady would not have spent the last eight years incarcerated. I am ashamed to be a part of a system that is apparently so lax." He glared at Page as if the entire thing were Page's fault. "I'm going to dismiss this case. The matter of whether she killed her husband and baby rightfully belongs in another court. This is no matter for the Capital Crimes Commission. Any discussion?" The judge glowered at Page, challenging him to respond.

"Yes," A.J. said. "I believe we may be doing the young lady a further injustice by returning jurisdiction to local courts. The Commission has her and by rights, we ought to see this thing through. I believe there is precedence."

"How can a dismissal do further harm?" Page said.

"Consider that she'll be forced to go through another full trial, unless of course, the local prosecutor wants to get off the hook with a lowered charge. In any case, she'll be ravaged by this procedure for the next two to three years, spending more time in jails, with the possibility of rape hanging over her head. She's already been raped once, by a guard, of all people. Let me try to find precedence. We owe her that much."

"Sir?" Pat said. "I'm sure I can find it rather quickly. I've just recently completed some course work having to do with this same subject. If memory serves, once the Commission enters into a case it can finish it even if the indicators of a capital crime are removed, providing the representation is licensed to practice within the state that has jurisdiction. I'm sure of it, and it won't take long to discover the appropriate case law."

The judge was silent as he thought the proposal over.

He looked at the three attorneys before him then over A.J.'s head at the young lady sitting at the defense table.

"Damn," the judge said. "Okay. Tell you what we're going to do. I'll commute the sentence immediately and announce that there is a motion before the court. The trial will be suspended, pending the results of that motion. I'll expect briefs to be filed not later than two weeks from today. I'll use one week to review, then I'll rule. Either for dismissal and return to a lower court or for a continuation. Any further discussion?" He looked from face to face. "Very well, let's have at it." He looked at Pat. "Young man, don't disappoint me."

8.

Back in A.J.'s hotel room, the defense team gathered for a small celebration. No champagne, but plenty of smiles - except for Bonnie.

Bonnie had not figured out what had happened. She thought it must be something pretty good, based on the reactions of the attorneys.

"Pat," A.J. said, "Have you any idea where you came across any reference to the Commission's jurisdiction in cases like this?"

"Sure do. It was one of the references I used in my doctorate work. Do you still have it with you? Check the footnotes. I found reference to it at the U of D library."

"Well, you better get cracking. Two weeks goes by before you know it. The rest of us deserve a little break." A.J. was smiling broadly.

"What do you mean, I better get cracking? I could use a little help here."

"Nonsense. You shot your mouth off. You can write the brief. The rest of us are going to party."

Finally, Britt noticed Bonnie.

"Bonnie," she said. "What's wrong? You certainly don't look as thrilled as I imagined."

"I don't even understand what happened," Bonnie said. "Why are all of you so happy?"

They all looked at her for a moment, then all began to laugh together.

"We had a big victory today," Britt said. "The judge commuted your sentence. That means you don't have to live in exile anymore."

"I'm innocent?" she said.

"Not exactly," Pat said. "That's the next step. ' What happened today is we proved you didn't shoot the man in the convenience store. With that proven, the Capital Crimes Commission really had no case with you. Therefore you shouldn't have been tried the way you had been, and never would have been exiled, even if you were guilty of everything else. Now we have to continue to see if we can prove your innocence in that regard as well."

She still looked a little puzzled.

"Here," A.J. said, holding both her hands. "If what had come out today, had come out eight years ago, you would not have had to go to trial at the federal level. Instead, you would have gone to court in Detroit. Hard to say how they would have handled that, but it's my guess they would have bargained the charges down to manslaughter. You would have gone to prison but would probably have been out in a year or so.

"Now, the judge wanted to just dismiss this case, and have you stand trial for the shooting of your husband and child back in Detroit. We said that would be a bad idea and would represent a cruelty to you. Pat here, thinks he can find a case that has already been accepted by the courts, which would allow us to finish right her in the same court, with the same judge and with the same jury. The judge is willing to give us some time to show him that it's okay to do that. He's allowed Pat two weeks to show him what that test case was. If Pat can do that, we'll go back to trial in three weeks, or possibly this trial will end and you'll have to start over in Detroit. Either way, it's better than what we started with and that's why we're so happy tonight. Understand?"

"I think so," Bonnie said. "While Pat's working we just have to hang around for the next two or three weeks?"

"That's right," Britt said.

"I'd like to go back while we wait."

"Go back?" A.J. said. "Back where?"

"Home. To Regenesis."

"Bonnie. You don't understand," Britt said. "You don't have to go back. Not now. Not ever." Britt started to smile till she saw tears welling up in Bonnie's eyes.

"But I have to. Lee. David. I have to." Bonnie could no longer speak. The tears were coming hard now.

"Jesus," A.J. said. "I forgot about your son. I fear we all forgot about him."

A.J. looked at each of them, trying to decide what to do.

"Damn. Looks like we've got work to do. And I'll bet the farm there's no precedent for this."

He called the judge at home and arranged for an evening meeting. When the judge objected to discussing anything to do with the case, A.J. offered to bring Page in, as well. The judge finally agreed. They met at nine that evening.

A.J. presented the situation as briefly and clearly as he thought he could, including the fact that he was sure there had been no precedent set. Page sat thoughtfully through the explanation, then slowly stood.

241

"Not only is there no precedent," Page said, "It doesn't even belong in this court. I suggest you take it to the Commission. In the meantime, since this doesn't concern me, you'll excuse me." He turned and left.

A.J. watched him go, then turned to the judge. "Your opinion?"

"He's right. It's a hell of a note, but even if I decided to take it on, the Commission would rule against me so fast, both our heads would be spinning... probably right off our respective necks. I'm sorry. Sorry for the girl, too. It's not her fault that we put her in this position." He shook his head and stared into his drink. "Make the calls, arrange whatever meetings you have to arrange. I'll go with you. Maybe together we can get a favorable ruling. I'll hold off reconvening till we've had our say with the Commission and get their ruling."

A.J. was left at the table alone.

9.

Pat had finished his brief and presented it. The following day, the judge ruled that it was within the Commission's jurisdiction to complete the trial. He also announced that the trial would be suspended pending the results of a petition to the Commission regarding dependents of the defendant. Privately, he told A.J. and Page that if the Commission's ruling took place more than thirty days from then, he would be forced to declare a mis-trial, based on the jury's inability to maintain focus after such a lengthy continuance.

The Commission had granted an emergency hearing to A.J. and A.J. was allowed to call the judge as a witness to the events he described. They had listened. They had retired to confer.

Six long hours later, they re-convened and requested a written brief. In recognition of the need for a timely response, they suggested that A.J. respond as quickly as possible. They would take only one day to review the document and would respond the following day. No deadlines had been set.

Rather than return to Michigan, A.J. elected to stay in the nation's capital and begin work immediately. Neither Pat nor Britt would be of any help to him. He rented a cubicle from a local computer service firm. They set him up with a voice recognition machine and he spent the next fourteen hours telling his story to a machine, which duly recorded his every word.

Pat, Britt, and Bonnie had returned to A.J.'s home and were waiting for word from him.

It was not quite dawn when he called. "Pat, fire up my computer. I'm going to download some documents. As soon as it's in, make a copy for both you and Britt. Don't work together. Take your time but don't dawdle. I need you to edit that thing. I've been operating on adrenaline for the last several hours and I'm afraid there might be some gibberish in that document. Edit, edit, edit. Make it smooth and as logical as you can get it. When you're as good as you can make it, let Britt have that draft and have her fix it up so it flows. And tell her I don't want one word in there that we can do without. Not one.

"I'm going to the hotel to catch some sleep. Don't call for at least six hours, but after that, call for anything. Anything at all that you don't understand or want to discuss.

"Oh yeah. I'll be at the Hyatt Regency, Capital Hill."

He hit a dozen keys, entered his home modem number, looked at the screen, then hit a return. "Damned wonderful machines," he said to no one.

There had been a number of calls between them over the next seventy two hours. They were all exhausted but they had finished the brief. It ended at page sixty three, double spaced. They had allowed one night's sleep, then read it again, made one more phone call to verify that it was their best effort, then A.J. called the Commission.

The Commission's panel had been surprised that the brief was ready. They re-arranged their schedule and asked A.J. if he could meet with them the following morning at nine. He could.

A.J. brought six copies with him and distributed them to the seated panel. No words were exchanged. A.J. sat in silence and watched the four men and two women reading. They all finished within minutes of each other. They put their heads together and murmured words A.J. couldn't hear.

Finally, the spokesperson, a woman barely in her sixties, addressed A.J. "Apparently there are no questions. At least not at this time. We must commend you on a superbly written document. You understand that is not a comment on the content, merely the quality of the presentation. We are also quite impressed with the timeliness of your delivery. We wish to respond in kind, naturally, but also, some among us feel that if we had a little more time to review, considering what is at stake..." She left the unfinished sentence trail as a question.

"I agree," A.J. said. "I wish I could say to take all the time in the world. However, this panel is aware of the deadlines we face and the consequences of an untimely response. Since we do have a little time, however, I would appreciate it if this panel would give as much time as it can spare to this matter."

"Thank you, Mr. Ripplestone. If you would leave word with the clerk where you can be reached for the next several days?"

A.J. half stood from his wheelchair and bowed toward the panel and left the room, feeling foolish for having bowed. He was still intimidated, after all these years.

He left his hotel name and number with the clerk and left the building. Sat in the sun for a few minutes and wished he could enjoy the next days. Better to be where I'm supposed to be, he thought. He took a cab the eight blocks back to the hotel.

Over the next four days, A.J. had made several phone calls to his home, just to tell them that nothing had yet happened and to ask after Bonnie. She was still depressed and spent most of her time sitting on the dock staring into the distance, Pat reported.

She had written several letters to David and asked Pat how to mail them. Pat didn't have the heart to tell her that her letters could not be delivered to Regenesis. He took them and promised that either he or A.J. would see to their delivery. And felt guilty about the lie.

A.J. told him he would have done the same thing.

In between calls to home, A.J. had contacted the Wayne County prosecutor, explaining the details of the case and inquiring as to what action might be taken, if any, should he be unsuccessful in continuing the trial under the Commission's jurisdiction. The prosecutor's initial reaction was not good. The man wanted to go for blood. After three more calls over the next two days, their conversation began to be more realistic and the prosecutor was beginning to ask more detailed questions and actually showed some sympathy for Bonnie's plight.

At the end of the third day, A.J. had called Pat and asked that everything that they had gathered be electronically mailed to the prosecutor in Detroit for his review. He hoped that by doing this the prosecutor may become convinced there would be no need for a trial, or at the very least to re-investigate before making any commitment for trial.

The waiting was beginning to get to A.J. He wished he were home doing something productive.

At the end of the third day, he called the Commission.

"Any word?" he asked the clerk.

"Not yet, sir. They're still in chambers."

On the fourth day, A.J. had picked up the phone six times and replaced the receiver each time without having made a call. He paced the suite in his wheelchair and found the large quarters much too small for his liking. He looked out the window at the fire station across the street. Ordered room service. Didn't eat.

It was nearly two when the phone rang. A.J. stared at the beige instrument willing it to betray the message by the tone of the ring, but its tone wouldn't change. On the fourth ring, he picked up. "Yes?" His voice didn't sound like his own.

"Mr. Ripplestone?" a female voice said.

"Yes. This is Ripplestone."

"Sir, the Commission panel would like to meet with you at four thirty this afternoon, if that's convenient for you?"

"Yes. Certainly," A.J. said. "Um... Miss? Have they indicated..."

"I'm sorry. I just got E-mail that asked me to call. I haven't spoken with anyone on the panel." She sounded sincere.

A.J. looked at his watch. Two hours. He called Pat, told him when they were scheduled for a meeting.

"They have questions?" Pat said.

"Oh, God. I don't know. I just presumed they had made a ruling." A.J. said he would call again as soon as he knew anything, replaced the receiver and began pacing the room in his chair, thinking that walking would help if his damned old legs worked better. The fire station was still outside the window.

10.

"It is not often," the chairperson said, "that this panel is reduced to a vote to make a decision, but in this case, it was necessary."

With that opening statement, A.J. believed he knew their findings. He heard little of what followed, although his gaze remained on the woman that was speaking and from all appearances, was attentive and concerned.

He remembered the day he committed to the law. He had only been nineteen years old. A mere puppy.

The early years were spent with a fervor akin to what those who choose a religious life must feel, he thought. He had been a prosecutor's assistant.

When had he chosen the Capital Crimes Commission? Oh, yes. He remembered. The Jesuit priest. The man seemed brilliant back then, when the world was full of black and white images. A.J. wondered if he had been brilliant enough to foresee Bonnie in all her shades of grey.

The chairwoman's voice seemed to fade in and out of consciousness. "...and as you are aware, genetic science has made wonderful gains in our lifetimes. Although there is still no scientific proof that there is genetic predictability for the criminal and violent behavior we are loath to witness, there has been enough established to warrant a view that coincidence is not the only thing at work. Even though Ms. White may prove to be innocent, there still remains the fact that her son has been sired by a man convicted of a violent crime, and while there is no absolute proof of a genetic disorder, the probability exists. It was for this very reason, that our predecessors established certain inviolable rules regarding the offspring of the criminally violent…"

Her voice had begun to fade.

How many years has it been, A.J. thought. More than a lifetime. How many appeals? Not enough. Not enough time, not enough energy.

He remembered the days when he had accepted cases based on merit, but not on belief. Until Bonnie, not one of the appeals he had handled generated any belief in innocence. It was only tactics.

Those years when he taught law. Did he teach from his heart or had he only been a tactician? When did he get so old?

"…are the considerations that bore upon us as we realized that a consensus was impossible. The vote, Mr. Ripplestone, was three to two."

A.J. glanced at his watch. Fourteen minutes. Only fourteen minutes. He looked at each of the panelists in turn. There was no indication of how they may have voted.

"Mr. Ripplestone?" the woman said, "speaking off the record, there is a consensus that there may be cause to consider the matter further and we might suggest an appeal is in order. We realize that the appeal process requires the best legal minds be brought to bear and that the process will require years of debate. This will be of no help to your client, but we sincerely hope that this subject does not remain closed. We thank you for bringing this matter to our attention and sincerely wish that we had the ability to…"

Her voice was replaced by A.J.'s thoughts, once again. My whole life... and what about Pat, Britt? This is wrong. The very core of my beliefs. Wrong.

It was the silence in the room that caused A.J. to realize the proceedings were over. He looked up and realized that he felt no compulsion to bow. He merely turned his chair and wheeled toward the oak doors.

When he arrived at his hotel, he sat in the middle of the room staring at the phone for a long time.

"Pat," he said into the mouthpiece, "I'll try to catch a flight first thing in the morning. I'll talk to Bonnie when I get there."

11.

A.J. landed in Detroit, switched airlines to a commuter flight that took him to Alpena. Pat picked him up at the airport. Britt had stayed with Bonnie.

"How is she?" A.J. said.

"She knows."

"What did you tell her?"

"Nothing. But she's not a stupid girl. What are our choices? Do you think we'll lose her to a lower court?"

"I'm not sure it will make any difference," A.J. said. "In my rush to prove innocence, I completely forgot the essence of the human element. She has a husband and a child back on the island. What must it be like for her to know we rejoiced in her inability to return to them."

"Perhaps we can arrange for her to re-join them," Pat said. "When a conviction is reached and sentence is passed, the courts always give the option to the family to join the prisoner. Now she's just the family trying to stay with her husband, the sentenced man. What do you think?"

"It's a good possibility. Might even get her out of a new trial. Before we begin meddling in her life again, let's ask Bonnie what she wants. If she wants to return, I'll do my best to see that it's possible. If she doesn't… well, we'll do our best to stay in the federal court and go for a full acquittal."

Pat turned onto the dirt road surrounded by forest that led to A.J.'s cabin and immediately swung into the weeds and brush to the side of the roadway, nearly hitting a large pine tree. An ambulance with lights flashing sped toward them. Behind the ambulance and almost invisible in the dust cloud was Britt's small foreign car.

She almost didn't see them, but at the last minute recognized the car and came to a sliding halt in the loose gravel. She pulled her car as far to the side as she was able and ran to Pat's car, jumping in the rear door.

"It's Bonnie!" She said.

Pat pulled out of the weedy shoulder and spun the car around in a 'U' turn. "What happened?" A.J. said. "Is she okay?"

"She hung herself. I never should have left her alone. In that tree down by the dock… I don't know… Hell! Alpena General, Pat."

A.J. twisted around in the seat. "Is she still alive?"

"Yes. But it's not good. I'm pretty sure her neck's broken. Her face was all blue and her eyes were… they were just huge!" Tears were streaming down Britt's cheeks and her adrenaline level was so high her whole body was jittering.

It was a forty five mile run to Alpena General Hospital and they drove at seventy five to eighty miles per hour for most of the distance.

They were still about twelve miles from town when the ambulance turned off its siren and began to slow to fifty five. "Why are they slowing down?" Britt said.

12.

The funeral was four days later. A.J. made the arrangements and notified family members. He also paid for the funeral.

There were only four persons that came to the service. A.J., Pat, Britt, and strangely, the judge.

A.J. had her cremated. It was the only way he could think of that would allow him to take her back to Regenesis.

The funeral director delivered her ashes to A.J.'s door in a brass urn. When the man left, A.J. placed the urn on the mantel of his fireplace and the three of them sat in the room staring at it but not speaking.

Finally, A.J. spoke. "Pat, I don't think I've ever been this tired. Yet, I have one more thing that I must do." He looked at both of them, sitting next to each other on the leather sofa. "Please make travel arrangements for me. I'd like to return Bonnie to Regenesis and I'd like to meet with her man, David."

He saw Pat about to speak and raised his hand to stop him. "I'll be going alone."

"Yes sir," Pat said.

After a time, A.J. addressed both of them. "There is one more thing that needs to be done and I'll rely on both of you to get it done. Go to the Commission. Appeal the ruling. Whatever it takes. Even if it's your life's work."

He wheeled himself toward his bedroom.

13.

A.J. made his trip to see David. Insisted on going into the compound to talk to David in his home. He died there.

I began to write this in an attempt to document my life's work to date in preparation for my teaching phase but I've been side tracked by Bonnie. She affected all our lives. Colored them, I suppose.

I begin teaching next month. It's not a rule of the Commission, but it's expected. When you reach sixty five. It's only fitting that we pass on our experiences to the new JDCC candidates.

I've worried about how I will teach. Bonnie affected me deeply. I'm still with the Commission. As a prosecutor. Britt filled A.J.'s role, the defense for appeals. Bonnie's influence, again, I'm sure.

By the way, Britt is my wife. Took almost twelve years for the first spark of romance to come into our lives. And when it did, it didn't grow into burning embers, or even burst into flames. It fairly exploded. We've been happy.

But I digress again. The point was to determine if I could teach. I needed to put my life into perspective.

I am an aggressive prosecutor, but because of Bonnie, I spend more time ensuring that the party is guilty than I do actually preparing and prosecuting the case. I know, I'm not the panel of judges. They determine guilt. But I'm so cautious…

Britt says that's what makes me a good prosecutor. But what would she know? She handles appeals.

Oh. We're still in debate regarding the future of children whose mother or father successfully appeals. But progress is being made.

And A.J.? The last thing he said to me was, "Boy, you've a good mind. Use it. But be sure you temper it with what's in your heart."

I guess that's the answer. When class begins, I'll teach law from that perspective.

Patrick S. Ripplestone, J.D.C.C.

About the Author

Jack Radtke was born in Michigan, married, and together with his wife, moved to northern Michigan in 1989. He began writing fiction shortly after and many of his stories use the small communities found there as a locale and highlight the residents of the area while allowing both the communities and the residents to remain anonymous. He and his wife remain residents of the area and his home is surrounded by woods and wildlife.

Printed in the United States
6404